COMBAT!

The Counterattack

A novel based on the
American Broadcasting Company Television Series

by Franklin M. Davis, Jr.

Illustrated by
Arnie Kohn

WHITMAN PUBLISHING COMPANY · Racine, Wisconsin

Dedicated to Foggy

and the

Citadel Class of 1966

CONTENTS

1

"THIS IS KEENO!"

Krauts were out there.

For sure.

Sergeant Chip Saunders, the squad leader, slid his steel helmet back a little so it wouldn't rasp on the stone wall of the cellar, then pressed against damp masonry to try to see out of what was left of the window. You hear noises, you better look, not just listen. It was a rule Saunders had learned the hard way in the fighting this far into France. Just because they were getting close to Germany didn't mean the war was over, not by the range of an M1 rifle.

Waving a grimy hand to Caje and Littlejohn to warn them not to move from where they were slumped in the corner behind him, Saunders bellied up to the window. Some trick of the light

9

from the fading sun seeping through the shell-fractured beams roofing the cellar gave Saunders a momentary glimpse of himself reflected in the broken glass of the windowpane. His taut disciplined face looked smudged with fatigue. The endless days and nights of battle action were marked on him, making him look older than his twenty-five years. Thin grooves that he'd never noticed before curved around his mouth. They gave him a grim expression, like he was going to spit any minute. Saunders dodged the reflection with a voiceless snarl, trying to get a good look out the window.

Now where was Kirby? That no-good fresh-faced kid was supposed to be squad security on this flank of the farmhouse, but you couldn't see him.

There was the noise again.

A faint click and rattle, like a rock rolling down a slope, sounded outside. Saunders caught up the rifle he carried now in preference to a tommy gun, the smooth wood of the balance reassuring him as he brought the piece up carefully to poke the muzzle through the window. *One shot is all I want,* he told himself. *One shot.*

Mentally, out of long habit, he reviewed his squad dispositions. Kirby outside, on the edge of the rubble heaped over the cellar if he was where he was supposed to be. Caje and Littlejohn just behind him, here in the cellar. Nelson on his way back to Lieutenant Hanley at the platoon CP to see about getting the ammunition they needed to replace the stuff they'd fired during the day. Brockmeyer spelling Littlejohn on the Browning Automatic Rifle, so Brock was posted to cover the farmhouse road behind them. Doc trying to organize some chow in what was left of the farmhouse pumproom. That was it. The squad. Saunders had been promised replacements for the rest of his men, but he sure wasn't holding his breath until they showed up.

So he had to do the job with what he had, the old Army game, and if anyone wanted to know, this flank outpost duty was for the birds. He'd had half a mind to tell Lieutenant Hanley that an understrength squad had no business pulling flank guard for the platoon for the night, even if the Krauts were pulling back. But the chance to grab a little rest for his men overruled Saunders' tactical judgment, so he'd kept quiet. Now he wished he hadn't. Outpost duty was rugged; you sat there with your belly muscles tight against the little arrows of fear shot at you by the oncoming darkness, the dank smell of the ruined cellar, and the enemy threat out there.

There was that noise again.

Saunders shoved the rifle butt hard against his shoulder and lowered his cheek to caress the stock as he flipped the safety off. Carefully, the yoke and drum sights looming big in his vision, he looked over the barrel of the rifle. Immediately in front of him the rubble was shoved against the wall, then sloped down into the farmyard where it rolled against a shed, a small outbuilding that looked like some kind of walled-up corncrib. Beyond, against the darkness falling fast now behind the lowering sun, the sweep of a broad meadow rolled in a gentle green wave to a tree line marking the road out of the village proper. During the day the squad, as part of the battalion attack, had pushed the Krauts back along that road and now the word was, *Button up for the night; hold what you got. We move on tomorrow.*

But a smart Kraut would keep probing at you, trying to keep you off balance, even if he was moving back. One thing Saunders had learned, don't think the Krauts were stupid. They were rough, tough combat soldiers. The American Graves Registration people had a truckload of filled mattress covers every day out of Saunders' own battalion to prove it.

"What you going to shoot at, Sergeant?"

A hoarse voice almost in his ear asked the question. Saunders, startled, said, "Kirby! I told you to stay where you could observe clearly! What are you doing there?"

"You getting nervous in the service, Sergeant?" Kirby was stooping down from the rubble pile just outside and above the cellar window, round face showing so much concern that Saunders was immediately suspicious. Kirby was a good man, just like they were all good men in the squad, but he was always putting his foot into something, fouling up the detail. When he looked like this, you'd better watch out.

"You check that noise, Kirby?" Saunders growled the question and pulled his rifle back through the window. "Or was that just you pussy-footing around up there when you were supposed to be on the alert?"

"You know me, Sarge. Always on the alert. Just like the book says." Kirby looked behind him, still stooping over, and then bent closer, this time a grin flitting under his button nose. "Send Caje or Littlejohn up here to relieve me. Got something to show you."

"What is it?"

"You'll see. I got to bring it down there. Send someone up."

Saunders turned away from the window, sent

Caje outside, and then squatted on an up-ended
fragment of cellar beam to light a cigarette. One
thing you had to hand Kirby; war or no war, he
was always up to something.

But Saunders almost swallowed his cigarette
when Kirby strolled through the sagging doorway, rifle slung over his shoulder, field jacket
and uniform sloppy as ever, and announced,
"Sarge, Littlejohn! You ready?"

"Ready for what, country boy?" Littlejohn,
lean as the rifle sloping against his outthrust leg,
scowled in annoyance. He caught Saunders' eye,
saying, "I thought we was going to get a little
sack time, Sarge. How come this ape is playing
games?"

"Games, my foot," Kirby said promptly. "We
got it made, Sarge, no stuff. This here's Keeno,
our new squad dog-robber!"

Kirby stepped aside and, with a gentle shove,
propelled a small figure into the middle of the
cellar.

Saunders' jaw dropped, Littlejohn snorted and

sat upright, and Kirby laughed. "That's right, you guys. Look at him. I got him signed up already. Ain't that so, Keeno?"

But Keeno didn't say anything. He stood half crouched, staring at Saunders out of huge black eyes, a boy about fourteen dressed in a peasant's smock like those they'd seen on civilians all around the place, faded gray stockings lumpy on his skinny legs, and dirty wooden shoes on his feet. He had a shock of long black hair brushed carelessly aside from a wide forehead, but his jaw was long with a narrow chin. With the impact of his eyes in his dead-white face he looked like a spooked pixie ready to vanish when someone said the magic word.

And Saunders said it. "Kirby, get him out of here!" He roared so loud the boy ducked as if he'd been struck, a matchstick arm coming up as if to protect himself.

"Aw, Sarge! Have a heart! I found the kid hiding in a hole in the rubble. He. . . ."

"Was that him making that noise?" Saunders

was thinking, the dumb kid, he might have gotten himself shot. Not much there to stop a .30 caliber steel-jacketed bullet. He was so skinny he looked like he hadn't eaten for a month. "Well, was it?"

"I guess so, Sarge." Kirby took a step nearer the boy. "I don't know what noise you mean, but he kept rolling little rocks at me. That's how I found him."

"Well, he's lucky he didn't get plugged." The sergeant got up off the beam, letting it clump to the floor. The boy jumped and moved toward Kirby, obviously for protection, his big eyes staring at Saunders.

"Now look, Kirby," Saunders went on, not looking at the boy, "I don't know what this is all about, but I'll tell you one thing. Get him out of here and get him out of here fast! You know the regulations as well as I do. No monkeying around with civilians."

"Aw, Sarge, listen!" Kirby patted the boy on the arm. "Keeno's a good kid. He's got no folks, no place to go, nothin'. And we're shorthanded, right? We don't know when we'll get any replacements, right? So Keeno can dog-rob for us; he can be orderly for the whole squad." Kirby, his own eyes gleaming now as he warmed to his speech, turned to Littlejohn. "Heck, the kid can wash Littlejohn's laundry, he can fix rations for us, he can scrounge for us, he can do a million things. We can fight this war like kings! He can—"

"The Army isn't drafting kids, Kirby." Saunders' voice was cold. He could tell from the way the kid's eyes flickered the kid was getting the message. "And even if we do, we're not going to begin with French kids who—"

"I'm trying to tell ya, Sarge! Gimme a chance!" Kirby interrupted sharply. "This kid's half English. Listen to him! Come on, Keeno, say hello to the Sergeant."

"How j'u do, Sergeant? I'm that pleased to meet you, sir. Truly I am."

Saunders' jaw dropped again. The kid spoke real English all right, honest-to-goodness Limey English in a high reedy voice like he'd just walked off a London street. The broad accent and the odd turn of phrase sounded out of place, unbelievable in a ruined cellar somewhere deep in France. Saunders took a deep breath, retrieved his cigarette, and started over.

"Okay, kid," he said gruffly. "Now give me the story from the beginning." Because he wasn't buying this, of course. A smart enemy would do very well to run a kid spy into the outfit. They knew what suckers Americans were for kids. What better gimmick than to infiltrate someone like this guy?

"Very well, Sergeant. I shall do my best." The boy stepped away from Kirby. With a passable imitation of coming to attention, he put his bony little hands alongside his legs, elbows pressing the smock, and said, "My name is Albert Quineaux. My father is a Frenchman of this village who was taken away by the Germans to work in Germany some months ago. My mother is English, and for a bit we lived in London before we came here to live." He smiled faintly, as if he didn't quite know how. Then he said, "I became separated from my mother when the mayor ordered the village evacuated but the Germans shelled us on the road."

Saunders bit into his cigarette, then threw it onto the floor. That made a good story, didn't it? A real tearjerker. He knew the Germans shelled refugee columns all right. He'd seen it happen a couple of times, as a matter of fact. But it was also a story to get your sympathy. You just couldn't forget that. "Okay, so they shelled the road. What happened to your mother?"

"I don't know, sir. I was that frightened, I ran here to hide when the shells started."

"So where's everyone else? If the mayor evacuated the whole village, where're the rest of the people?"

The boy shrugged. Now the pixie face looked haunted and he seemed to be looking at something over the sergeant's shoulders. "That I do not know, sir."

The sergeant wiped a hand along his jaw. No

matter how tempted he might be to help this kid,
there was only one way to play it. Send him back
through channels to Battalion S-2 and let the
Intelligence people there decide what to do with
him. After all, this was a squad of combat infantry
fighting a shooting war that took men, good men.
A kid couldn't do anything but louse it up.

"Okay. What do they call you—Keeno? Okay,
Keeno, get ready for a little trip. I'll send you up
the line to battalion. They'll figure out what to do
with you."

The boy's mouth worked a little and it struck
Saunders that maybe the kid was too proud to
ask for anything to eat. "You found him, Kirby,"
he said, "you feed him. Give him a box of K
rations or something." Then as Kirby started to
say something Saunders went on. "Now don't
fight the problem, hotshot. I'm running this squad.
I say he goes back to battalion."

"Aw, Sarge, for the love of Mike. This kid can
help us. He already said he would. Didn't you,
Keeno? Tell him."

As the boy nodded Saunders exploded, "I don't care what he says! No civilians with this squad. It's a security risk along with everything else. The lieutenant would fry me in deep fat if he thought we were using kids. This isn't a ding-dong Sunday-school picnic, Kirby. It's a war. It's no place for kids. You got that? Okay. Now get him out of here. Take him over to the platoon. And while you're at it, tell Nelson to get back on over here. I want to get organized for the night."

But the words were hardly out of his mouth before Nelson loped through the door, a rangy well-muscled soldier who somehow always managed to look neat and tidy no matter how muddy and dirty the rest of them got. He had a round, rather youthful face that didn't quite match the rest of him, as if his head had been made for someone else and handed to him by mistake. So it was easy to forget that Nelson was a good tough doughboy; you always wanted to pat him on the top of those blond curls. Now he said, a little out of breath, "Hey, Sarge. Hey! The lieutenant says to form up and join the column on the road. We're moving out. Right now. We're gonna make a night attack. He'll issue the orders on the march."

"Dag-nab it, what kind of a way's that to fight a war?" This from Littlejohn, still flaked out in the corner.

"Quiet, you." Saunders growled at him, then told Nelson, "Okay, I got you. Pass the word to Doc, Caje, and Brockmeyer outside. You get any dope on the ammunition?"

"I brought one case. It's outside. There'll be more later when we get the supply up tonight."

As Nelson went out to get the others, Saunders turned to Kirby. "Now, as for this kid. Leave him here, you understand? That's an order, Kirby. You got it?"

Kirby looked at him for a long time, his dark face very solemn. "Yes, sir, Sergeant, sir. I got it, sir."

Saunders compressed his lips. Kirby was over-doing it, of course. Well, if the squad got the platoon point, he'd put Kirby out in front. Let the dark and the belly-knotting fear shape him up. That'd teach him to get wise. And to the boy Saunders said, "Sorry, Keeno. But there's a war on. You know? Now shove off."

2

"I WAS TRYING TO HELP!"

Outside, as the squad formed up in a loose column, Saunders said, "Okay, sound off roster check. Make sure we got everybody. Brockmeyer . . . Caje . . . Doc . . . Kirby . . . Littlejohn . . . Nelson . . . okay."

Saunders hesitated for a moment, wanting to tell the squad that he hated to rout them out from what was the best billet they'd had in days even if it was a ruined farmhouse. But it was an old rule with him, and a good one, never to apologize for an order. Like he'd told that kid—Keeno?—there was a war on. They all knew it. An order was an order. It was a sacred thing. You got told to do something, you did it. Apologize for it, soften it in any way, and you got a halfhearted weak-sister performance in execution. And that wasn't how

25

Sergeant Saunders ran his squad.

But at the same time, these guys weren't machines. Saunders knew they were tired, bone tired, with the fatigue that grabbed you like a big hand in the seat of the pants and tried to pull you down, down, down into some soft darkness where you could rest in a sleep you wanted so badly you could taste it. When you were that woofed, your combat effectiveness went down because people got careless, sloppy. They got the yips so that at dusk, like now, they might get clobbered. You had to watch out for that.

Around them the French countryside looked soft and friendly. The rolling land had a pleasant cast emphasized by the way the oncoming darkness smoothed out the raw fractures of the war. The ruined buildings lost their sores in shadows; the ditch that only that morning held a blazing Kraut machine gun was invisible and harmless now. Even the road, full of ruts and potholes, looked like a silvery ribbon as it wound toward the tree line ahead. There was a deceptive quiet lying over the land, as if the night, not far now behind the setting sun, was throwing a blanket over the noise and violence of the day. Saunders knew this was an illusion, and because Nelson had brought word of a night action coming off, he knew it was only a matter of hours before the squad would be caught up in the torrent of combat again. So he spoke briskly, gruffly, saying, "Okay, you guys. Quick equipment check . . . packs . . . individual weapons? Okay. Littlejohn, you got the BAR? Good. Brock, you keep my tommy gun; I'll hang onto this rifle for now."

Saunders looked along the road toward the tree line where he could see the rest of the platoon and part of the company snaking out of the positions and moving out, so he went on. "I'm going up to get the word from the lieutenant. Kirby, you take squad point for now. Caje, you're assistant squad leader, you got command until I rejoin." He paused. Fixing them collectively with a hard stare, he said, "And no funny stuff with that kid Keeno. I told you to get him out of here and I meant it. Got it?" When nobody said anything, just stared back, Saunders said, "Right. Okay, column of twos on either side of the road, action interval. I'll rejoin you at the tree line. Move out."

Lieutenant Hanley's instructions were brief. Too brief, Saunders thought. A night attack was about as hairy a deal as you could pull. The book said you did it with lots of prior reconnaissance and you went for a close-in objective. You even rehearsed it if you had the chance, over terrain as similar as you could find. But there was lots about war that was different from the book, and this was one of those times.

"Battalion wants to smooth out the regimental line," the lieutenant said. "If we don't, the Krauts may come on back in tonight and we'll lose all we got today." He looked at his watch, a young fresh-faced man with the gold bars of a second lieutenant on the shoulder loops of his field jacket and his equipment—combat pack, map case, field belt, and carbine—riding snug and tight on his trim body. But his combat boots were old, wrinkled, and worn, the sure sign of a working infantry officer. "I make it about an hour to full dark," he said, looking up from his watch to face his three rifle squad leaders and the attached weapons squad men. "We'll go forward on Recon now, but take a look at my map first."

The group moved to a flat grassy spot under the trees and as Lieutenant Hanley unfolded his map case and laid it out on the ground, they knelt to follow the lines and contours his finger traced. "We're here now. We move out along this main road, and the platoon takes up an attack position out here, on the forward slope of this little knoll. The attack objective is this little high-ground crossroads village here. It's maybe a thousand yards straight down this pole line. That's the axis of the attack. Now, our platoon is support platoon and we may not even get into the action. The Battalion CO thinks if we jump quick before the Krauts set their night security, we got it made. So the company less our platoon attacks straight down the pole line. Got that?"

The crouching squad leaders nodded, murmuring approval. You needed a well-defined axis for a night attack. A pole line was okay. A railroad track would have been even better.

"Okay," the lieutenant went on, his dark eyes roving over the group and his words coming in his clipped style. "Now two important things. Be sure everybody, and I mean everybody, understands this. The first thing is, we've got to have absolute quiet. Don't even let 'em breathe. Absolute quiet. That clear?"

Saunders nodded with the rest of them. Noise carried at night. A lot farther than you'd ever think. And because surprise was so vital to the success of night action in particular, this was a worthwhile and necessary precaution. They'd have an assembly-position halt to check all loose or rattling gear. That was S O P—standard operating procedure—in the platoon.

"Now the next thing. The signal for the jump-off is a string of amber flares. They'll go off straight up at twenty-two hundred. The Division

Artillery will plaster the objective, we can get all four battalions if we need it, and—question, Saunders?"

"Yes, sir." Saunders tapped the map. "Does the platoon get a forward observer for the artillery, or do we call in our own fires? We have to know the check points and concentration numbers if we don't get the observer himself."

"That's right. But the company commander thinks he can make this with two platoons and we may not even get in the act." Lieutenant Hanley grinned quickly, showing excellent teeth. "That doesn't make anyone mad, does it?"

The group muttered a responsive chuckle, and the lieutenant went on. "Anyway, the deal is, there'll be one artillery observer with the company commander, but the jump-off concentration goes off immediately after the amber flares. Now, if the Old Man commits us, we'll use the walkie-talkie to call for any artillery fire support we need. I'll have the fire-plan numbers by then. Okay so far?"

"Yes, sir," Saunders said. "I'm with you."

Lieutenant Hanley then assigned the squad missions, finishing by saying to Saunders, "Your squad pulls flank security for the platoon and the company. That means you got the right flank for the whole attack if we don't get committed. If we do get committed, turn the mission over to a BAR team and. . . ."

"Leave my weapons support behind?" Saunders asked the question incredulously. "That doesn't make much sense, Lieutenant."

"Maybe not, but that's how we have to do it. The whole point of the night attack now is to do it quick and get the objective on the cheap. I frankly think there won't be any trouble."

The assembled squad leaders exchanged glances. They'd all heard that before. And it never worked out that way. But at the same time, Saunders knew they had to do it like this. He'd spoken his piece, the lieutenant expressed the decision, and now like a good soldier, Saunders would support it. That was the Army way. So all

Saunders said was, "Yes, sir. I hope you're right."

And it didn't shape up too badly. Not in the beginning. Saunders completed his reconnaissance, checked possible routes forward from the flank position that he might have to use later, and by nine o'clock, when it was solid dark, they were in support position, Littlejohn and his BAR covering the most likely avenues of enemy approach to the right, the balance of the squad tucked in against a junction of two stone walls that gave them an extra sense of security against the pressure of the night.

Saunders had beat the squad over the head so hard with the need for absolute silence that as they hugged the wall and sweated out ten o'clock, the only sound Saunders could hear was his own breathing. The moon was a bare sliver in the sky overhead, and most of the stars were obscured with cloud drift, but as he looked around him, the darker lumps against the stone wall could be identified readily enough, which meant his control would be simplified.

Saunders hated night attacks, as most soldiers did, because the war was bad enough in daylight without trying to fight it in the dark. On the other hand, he recognized the value of taking this particular objective; it would make future movement of the battalion and the larger forces they belonged to—Regiment, Division, Corps and so on —easier. In many ways, fighting a war was like fighting a boxing match. If you could keep your good punches going, you could win the round. The Battalion, as the principal large tactical unit of Saunders' immediate world, represented one of several fists of the Division. Getting this objective and smoothing out their position would let them throw more fists in better style tomorrow and the next day and the day after that until eventually the Krauts were finished and the war was won.

So for a long moment he concentrated on the details of the operation in front of him, barely noticing the fresh moist smell of the French earth around him, hardly aware that it was a pleasant velvety night, almost warm for that time of the year. He was glad in a way, now, that the squad had the flank security mission. In these night attack circumstances, it was a better deal than going forward behind the artillery concentration, your belly tied in knots, nothing but the light of fire and shell burst to see by, confusion and terror piling around you no matter how well the attack got off.

As he always did in these circumstances, he reviewed Lieutenant Hanley's orders to be sure nothing had been left undone.

Absolute silence. Yeah, that was okay. You didn't have to tell these guys twice about the need for quiet. They'd stacked loose gear in the assembly position for Doc to bring up later. Around them, the only noises were the night sounds— a gentle pulsing of the darkness, a softness of breeze, and only occasionally the rustle of clothing or the beat of a breath.

Walkie-talkie. Okay. Caje had that now, almost at Saunders' elbow, and they were in the net, but on listening silence. No communications until jump-off at ten, about what? Saunders checked his watch, carefully screening the radium dial with his sleeve—yeah, thirty-five minutes from now.

Fire-plan numbers. On the head. The map inside Saunders' shirt had key positions circled and numbered. In a pinch, the squad could ask for artillery fire on a number of places in the objective area and around its approaches by calling through the company radio net: *"Fire Number Thirty-two!"* Then, *Barrrooooom!* down would come the artillery. It was as simple as that, once you had it all laid on.

Ammunition. That was S O P—standard. Issue necessary ammunition in the assembly area, and they'd done that with the stuff supply brought up—Ammunition! Saunders mentally kicked himself. Then with a quick pat on Caje's shoulder to let him know he was moving, Saunders crawled down the stone wall to Nelson.

Putting his mouth close to Nelson's ear, Saunders whispered, "Where's that ammunition you brought down this afternoon?"

Even in the dark, Saunders could tell Nelson was surprised at the question. He drew in his breath with a sharp gasp, and the smudge of his face looked startled. Saunders repeated the question again, very low. Somewhere beyond them would be Kraut listening posts. You couldn't be too careful. "Who's got the ammo?"

Nelson shook his head. Then he whispered, "Not me, Sarge. I think Brock."

Mentally growling, Saunders scuttled down the wall to Brockmeyer, then to Kirby, even to Littlejohn at the BAR. Sweating now, he had the answer. *Nobody had picked up the case. They'd left it behind.*

Back at his own spot next to Caje, Saunders silently removed his helmet and wiped the sweat off his forehead. His clothes felt suddenly damp and sticky, not so much from crawling over the whole squad position, but from the anxiety sluicing through his belly. What a boner! What a fluff! Leaving ammo behind!

Saunders shook his head, then put his helmet back on, carefully leaned his head against the stone wall so the helmet wouldn't click and tried to think. What to do? It was Nelson's responsibility, of course. But it was Saunders' own fault for not double-checking it when they moved out. It was more than just losing the ammo and the possibility the Krauts might find it. If the squad got committed, they'd *need* it.

Saunders checked his watch, trying to decide if he should send Nelson back after it. But it would take him an hour or more, round trip. The attack was due off in fifteen minutes now. The squad could be committed and—Saunders gulped—all dead before Nelson ever got back. On the other hand, if you took a chance on going with what they'd been issued from Supply, maybe you could make it, maybe not. Saunders cursed himself. He wasn't worth his stripes!

"Sarge. Sarge!" The voice in his ear was Brockmeyer, relaying a message from Littlejohn at the BAR. "Something out on the road to our right rear. Littlejohn says for you to come out!"

Saunders ground his teeth. Trouble already. He'd have to forget the missing ammunition and deal with this. He wormed his way over the wall and along the slope to where Littlejohn had the BAR covering the slope and the distant road, now a faint ribbon in the dark. Littlejohn tapped Saunders on the shoulder and gestured toward the road, jabbing a forefinger.

Saunders nodded, removed his helmet, and pressed his head close to the ground. *Clip-clop. Clip-clop.* Someone was coming up the road!

Saunders raised his head, put his face close to Littlejohn's and held a finger to his mouth for silence. Together they listened again. *Clip-clop. Clip-clop.* The noise was louder now, you could hear it plainly without putting your ear to the ground.

What was it?

Krauts!

Clip-clop. Clip-clop.

Krauts?

Saunders stared down at the road. Then, not believing his eyes or his ears, he fumed wordlessly as two things happened. Along the road, as if he were strolling down a London street, wooden shoes clattering to wake the dead, came Keeno.

Gripped in his arms as if it would fly away was the ammunition case. "I say, Kirby! *Kirby!* Mr. Kirby, sir!" Keeno's choir-boy voice burst across the night like a thunderclap. "You forgot some equipment, sir. Where are you, sir? I've fetched it for you. Oh, Mr. Kirby. Where are you, sir? I have your parcel."

That tore it. Suddenly the night was ripped apart by giant claws. *Oom-poom-poom. Oom-poom-poom! Duh-duh-duh-duh-duh-duh-Wham!* Kraut firepower opened up, blasting the attack position, slamming into the squad, carving up the darkness in great gusts of flame and arching tracers. *Duh-duh-duh-duh!*

"Cover, everybody!" Saunders screamed the order at the squad, and took a flying dive over the wall to Caje, grabbing the walkie-talkie.

Squeezing the rubber cut-in switch with both hands, Saunders bellowed into the mouthpiece even as the ground slammed and roiled under him. But he couldn't raise Lieutenant Hanley.

Wordlessly, the anger a sour spume on his tongue, Saunders crouched against the wall, taking the pounding with the rest of the company and the squad. With every *oom-poom-poom,* with every *duh-duh-duh* of the incredible cyclic rate of Kraut machine guns, Saunders said to himself, over and over, *"Keeno did it on purpose, he did it on purpose!"*

Keeping one ear to the walkie-talkie, covering the other against the horrendous sounds of the slamming fire, Saunders heard the American attack jump off early. Orders crackled on the radio net. Overhead, like punctuation marks against the sky, the amber flares strung out. *Pop-pop-pop.*

Above them now was the high wailing whistle of the outgoing American artillery. As the big shells slammed into the objective the German fire

gradually lessened, shifting from prearranged
targets to targets of opportunity as the attack went
home. Looking over the stone wall toward the
pole line and the high ground ahead, Saunders
could see the holocaust of the night, fires swelling
to silhouette the darting soldiers of the attack
wave, an occasional ricochet tracer moving lazily
through the night with an illusory grace. The
ground shook and vibrated. The sounds of action
ripped and snarled across the countryside.

In the crackling radio traffic, Saunders followed
the fight, convinced that because the Germans
had been alerted by Keeno's incredible action, the
attack would fail. Once he said, "Nelson! Go back
and get Doc! Send him forward. Company's got
plenty casualties. They can use him!"

Saunders' eyes smarted as he thought of the
men wounded by the compromise of the surprise,
good men who otherwise might have made it if
Keeno hadn't pulled this. "Kirby. *Kirby!* You go
find that little so-and-so if you have to bring him
in spitted on the end of a bayonet like a ding-dong

weeny roast! I want that kid *here!*"

Then, at first slowly, and later with incredible swiftness, a curtain of silence fell on the night. The darkness was still punctuated with an occasional shell burst or the flutter of small-arms fire, but the radio traffic indicated the objective was being secured. Because Saunders couldn't understand why neither his platoon or squad had received orders to join the disrupted attack, he grabbed his rifle and loped forward through the night to find Lieutenant Hanley.

The officer was right where he said he'd be, at the double telephone pole carrying the junction box.

"What gives, Lieutenant?" Saunders flopped down beside him as Lieutenant Hanley handed the radio he'd been using to Dingervitch, his runner. "They need us, don't they?"

"No sweat, Saunders, near as I can tell. It got a little hairy there for a minute when the First Platoon hit a Kraut listening post that came moving in on the edge of their attack position.

That made us jump early. But it went okay. No orders for us yet."

Saunders stared at him, disbelieving. Nothing would convince him that it wasn't Keeno with his big feet in those wooden shoes and that long-range voice that nearly ruined them all. But he knew better than to tell the lieutenant his impressions because it would make the whole squad look bad, so he contented himself with asking, "Any orders for us?"

The lieutenant nodded. "Button up in place. You keep the flank security mission. Get a runner over here to me for tying in the contact and later on Supply will get the bedrolls up." He grinned quickly. "And tell your braves I promise them a hot breakfast. I told you this one wasn't going to be any trouble, didn't I?"

"Not for us, maybe. But I got the word on the walkie-talkie we were taking plenty casualties. I sent Doc on forward."

Lieutenant Hanley shook his head. "Not many. You know how it is. You always think you get more than you actually do get until you make a careful check. We had a few wounded, and at least four killed. But that's not bad for this kind of attack."

Saunders nodded and headed back to the squad. *Not bad for this kind of attack.* You got that way about casualties, almost had to. If you worried too much, you couldn't ever order a man to do the things you had to do in combat. So the lieutenant's attitude was easy to understand because it was the only attitude you could take and keep your sanity and effectiveness. But at the same time, Saunders was convinced, there were guys sleeping in mattress covers tonight who wouldn't be there if it weren't for that little clot Keeno.

"Where is he?" Saunders fired the question at Kirby when he got back to the squad position.

Kirby looked at Saunders for a long moment, then said slowly, "Look, Sarge, take it cool, huh? The kid was really trying to help us, honest he was. He was really trying to help."

"Trying to help us? Have you lost your ever-loving mind? He was trying to help the Krauts!"

Littlejohn loomed beside them in the dark. "Come on, Sarge," he wheedled. "Take five. Grab a smoke. We got a blackout shelter rigged in the wall junction there. Calm down. The kid didn't mean it."

Saunders stared at him, putting his helmet so close to Littlejohn's there was a click of steel. *"Where's that kid?"*

"In the blackout."

Saunders groped his way into the blackout rig, a little four-sided lean-to of shelter halves and blankets, a flashlight with the blackout screen removed providing a little light. Keeno huddled against the stone backdrop, big eyes wider than ever in the faint light, his triangular face streaked. Beside him, crouching on the missing ammunition case, was Nelson.

"Okay, Keeno," Saunders said as he knelt down and dug for a cigarette. "Your little plan failed, didn't it? The Americans have the objective."

Keeno looked at Saunders, then at Nelson, the

sound of his breathing quick and harsh. "I—I don't twig, sir."

"You heard me. You came stomping down that road in those wooden clodhoppers and tried to signal the Germans. You almost made it."

Keeno rubbed a hand quickly over his smock. "But you forgot this, sir. This box. It is ammunition. I thought you would need it. I was trying to help you, sir."

"He's right, Sergeant." Nelson spoke up. "I can prove—"

"Now listen, you." Saunders interrupted, pointing his finger at Keeno but taking in Nelson with his tone. "I told you before to shove off. I meant it. You're lucky I don't have you shot. You could have blown the gaff on this whole attack. What's more, I think you meant to. So you be out of here by the time I come to in the morning. That clear? Okay."

Then, speaking to Nelson, Saunders gave him some quick instructions for buttoning the squad up for the night, finishing with, ". . . I'm sacking out. You know the S O P. Get me up if something comes off. Otherwise standard security drill. Got that, Nelson?"

When Nelson nodded wordlessly, Saunders ground his cigarette out in the grass, picked up his rifle and wriggled out of the blackout. He found a reasonably soft spot along the edge of the wall, and rigged his field jacket for a pillow. His last conscious memory before he fell asleep was hearing Nelson whispering to someone, " . . . and Sarge means it. What we gonna do about Keeno, anyway?"

Saunders grinned sleepily. He'd sure answered that one for them, hadn't he?

3

"A KID SPY!"

Saunders awakened before daylight, a long habit acquired by the necessities of war. Even though he was a little stiff from sleeping on the ground, Saunders went automatically about the quickest of morning routines while he checked the squad out with a practiced eye.

Positions okay, but something was up. He could sense it. He massaged his scalp vigorously, then dug his toothbrush out of his pack, squeezing almost the last of his toothpaste on the brush with one hand while he unstoppered his canteen with the other. Time enough for a shave later when—

"Here you go, Sarge." Kirby, grinning, put a helmetful of hot water in a socket of rockets at the wall and then handed him a canteen cup of steaming coffee. "Breakfast in the rack. Pretty keen, hey? No pun intended."

Sipping the coffee gratefully, Saunders eyed Kirby, then said, "The minute I woke up I knew something was going on. What is it?"

Kirby grinned again. "Relax, Sarge. No strain."

"Come on, give."

"You won't like it."

"Don't spare me. Give."

Kirby squatted on his heels, looked earnestly at Saunders, then fished two four-packs of cigarettes out of his jacket pocket and stuffed them into Saunders' field jacket. "Courtesy of the mess sergeant. No charge."

"Come on, quit stalling. What's up?"

Kirby took a deep breath. "Keeno's still here."

When Saunders spluttered in his coffee, Kirby said, "I told you you wouldn't like it. But no stuff, we couldn't help it. A Kraut company's closed in behind us. During the night. We're cut off, just about. We had no place to send the kid."

Saunders set the coffee cup down carefully,

fixed Kirby with a stare, then said, "For a guy that's cut off, you sound almost happy about it."

Kirby shrugged. "You know this hubba-hubba outfit. The poor Krauts, they got us surrounded."

Saunders waved a hand, taking in the coffee cup, the squad-feeding utensils arrayed near the blackout rig, the several helmets of hot water he could see, and the men crouching in various attitudes of eating or shaving. Nobody looked very excited; instead they all looked somehow relaxed and content, so he said, "And all this is courtesy of Keeno, hey? Instead of going down by infiltration, squad combat feeding routine and all that jazz, we got ourselves a Number One boy, just like those Marines in China before the war, is that it?"

"You got to admit it works pretty good."

For a moment Saunders thought of dumping his coffee out as a sign of his fury, then decided that the coffee tasted too good to waste in a futile gesture like that. Instead he said casually, not letting on to Kirby what he really thought, "Now

tell me more about this Kraut company that has us cut off, buddy-ro. Like what strength, what weapons, how are they disposed, what are we doing about them?"

Kirby tried to pull it off, but he couldn't. His good-humored face broke up in a series of wrinkles and he guffawed out loud. "You don't fool easy, do you, Sarge? That's right. They're prisoners. We bagged practically a whole company in the attack last night. Back there's the POW pick-up point."

"And that's no place to send a growing boy who might be influenced by such evil associations, right?"

"Right, Sarge."

Swiftly, Saunders shot out a hand and gripped Kirby by the slack of his jacket, twisting it against his chest. "Now you get this, Kirby, and get it mighty, mighty quick. I gave an order, didn't I? Then it's your job as well as everyone else's to see that it's obeyed, is that clear?" Saunders dropped his hand, then, with a gentle tone just the reverse of the growl he'd given Kirby, he said, "So get rid of the boy, man. Right now."

"Can't."

"What do you mean, 'can't'?"

"Because we just sent him to Supply to lug the bedrolls over and here he comes back. With Lieutenant Hanley."

Saunders jumped to his feet, almost kicking over his coffee. He brushed off his jacket, then went forward to greet Lieutenant Hanley, carefully ignoring the questioning glances of the squad members scattered along the wall.

"Good morning, sir." Saunders gave the lieutenant the daily salute they confined themselves to in the combat zone. Ignoring Keeno who stood a pace back of the officer, Saunders said, "We got the hot chow you promised. And I won't say we weren't mighty glad to see it, because we were."

"Oh, that? Yeah, okay," the lieutenant said. "Listen, what's the story on this kid? You mind if I borrow him a little while?"

"Borrow him?" Saunders couldn't keep the

surprise from his voice. "I've been trying to bounce him out of here ever since late yesterday afternoon. But he doesn't bounce too easy." Saunders almost added, "Thanks to the yahoos in this squad!" But he didn't. You never knocked your own men to the brass. It was bad leadership. Both Lieutenant Hanley and Saunders knew it. "You can have him to keep."

"Well, I don't want to do that. He seems to think he belongs to your squad. But anyway, the thing is, we got a big bag of prisoners last night and the Battalion S-2 is trying to give them a preliminary screening back there before they get evacuated to Division. This kid speaks German pretty well he tells me. He could help—"

"Brockmeyer speaks German, Lieutenant." Saunders thought it ridiculous to give Keeno any more chances to foul things up. "I'd rather send him."

"Yeah," Lieutenant Hanley said reasonably. "But then you give away one of your effectives. We may be moving out again pretty quick. Let's send the boy over. You mind?"

Saunders kept his self-control with an effort. He reminded himself that he'd get rid of Keeno yet, even if the kid seemed to charm everyone else in sight. "Yes, sir," he said stiffly. "I'll give him some instructions."

"Don't trouble yourself. I've got to go over there. There may be some hot stuff we can use today. I'll take care of it." The lieutenant started to move off, Keeno trotting happily behind him while Saunders scowled at his flapping wooden shoes. Then Lieutenant Hanley turned and said, "Go ahead and finish chow, do any cleaning up you can, and stand by for orders. I ought to have something firm in an hour or so."

"Yes, sir."

As soon as the lieutenant, Keeno trailing, went on down the slope Saunders vaulted back over the stone wall and assembled the squad, less Brockmeyer who was spelling Littlejohn on the BAR again and had to stay in position. Saunders perched on the wall and retrieved his coffee cup.

When the squad members were all watching him he waited an extra moment, then started.

"You can't say I'm not a reasonable man," he said, "and I prove this by the fact we got this far and you clowns are still alive. As a squad we've done pretty well. We're a good military unit. We live, eat, and drink combat, and that's why we're good at it. And I'll tell you again, like I've told you about fifty times already, that kid Keeno is dangerous. My mind is made up. But because I'm a reasonable man, I'll give anyone that wants it a chance to speak. We're going to settle this Keeno business today, once and for all. I won't have my authority and this squad undermined by a skinny kid in a goofy artist's shirt. But because you all are so obviously set on him, I'll give you each a chance to express your opinions about Keeno. So sound off. Okay, you first, Caje, you're assistant squad leader."

Caje studied the tips of his fingers, tugged at the black beret he always wore, then said in his faintly accented voice, "It is the simple arithmetic with me, Sergeant. We are short one man in the squad, two when you count that Doc is an attached medic. The boy wants to stick with us. Let him, I say. A good worker, he is. Took all the bedrolls back to Supply in one trip. He will help the squad."

"Never mind if he almost snookered up that attack last night, him and those big feet. 'Mr. Kirby, sir, I have your parcel.' Okay, Kirby, you started this." Saunders nodded at the man. "You next, Mr. Kirby, sir."

Kirby's round face was solemn. "I told you at the beginning the kid could be a dog-robber. Look what he done already. He rustled hot water, he carried in the squad chow, he already started washing our mess gear when we had to send him to Supply to get the bedrolls back and the lieutenant grabbed him off."

Saunders shook his head. "The first target of any agent is going to be the brass, that ought to be obvious even to you birds. Okay, Nelson, you got the wiggles. What's your comment?"

Nelson blew a long plume of cigarette smoke. "I tried to tell you last night I could prove the kid was what he said he was, only you wouldn't let me." Nelson pulled a small satchel, a cheap-looking brief case, from under his legs. "Here's Keeno's ditty bag. Lemme show you."

"That the kid's personal stuff? You shouldn't go rooting around in there, Nelson."

"Ain't much here, Sarge. Keeno's traveling pretty light, you know. After all, the Krauts handled him and his town pretty rough. His mother, too, I guess. And they've got his old man." Nelson opened Keeno's little satchel and shook it. A packet of papers, a pair of socks, a comb, and a ragged toothbrush were all that fell.

Well, it was a pitiful collection of personal gear all right. Saunders would give him that. But on the other hand, none of them was exactly traveling first class either. "What're those papers, Nelson?"

"I'll show you." Nelson untied the packet carefully, then riffled through the little heap. "A French passport with British visas showing his name is Albert Quineaux, mother Doreen Quineaux, father Pol Quineaux. Arrived in France about four years ago, age ten then, fourteen now, of course. The stamps show he was about seven years in England. A letter on some very cheap paper, telling him his father Pol Quineaux is thought to be in a German forced labor camp around Wesel in Germany. A fancy sheet that I think is his folks' French marriage license. Some kind of diploma from school, pretty good grades if I read it right. And about four bucks in French money."

"So?" Saunders shifted his leg on the rocks. "The best thing Krauts do is forge papers."

Suddenly the squad started talking all at once.

"... Helped me roll my pack". . . "Strong little kid for all he looks so skinny" . . . "Poked me awake once when I almost fell asleep on guard last night". . . "Knows how to clean a rifle—"

"Wait a minute. *Wait* a minute!" Saunders held up a hand for quiet. "You all want him to stay, don't you?"

"That's right, Sarge!" Virtually as one man, the squad chorused its reply.

"Okay, here's the decision. I don't care what you guys say. There's nothing I ever see in Army Regulations that says you guys are entitled to a dog-robber anyway. That's for field officers. Big brass. Lieutenant Hanley doesn't even have one. So the kid goes as soon as we can get him out of here. That clear?" Saunders got up off the wall and gently nudged Keeno's belongings with his toe. "As soon as he gets back, give him his stuff and his ditty bag. Get him out of here. That's the end of it. Understand?"

Nobody said anything, but looking at their faces, Saunders knew they'd never understand his attitude. They saw him as a monster, an unfeeling martinet who hurt kids and robbed them of their comfort. Well, he told himself, never mind. They got mad at me in basic when I made them sweat. They've seen now why it was a good thing. They'll understand this someday.

But because he didn't really enjoy rubbing their

noses in the unpopular decisions any more than he enjoyed the making of them, Saunders tried to get the reasoning through. "Keeno's a security risk. You'll thank me for this someday. So like I said, that's the end of it. Now everyone back on the stick. We'll be moving out before long."

But that wasn't the end of it. By the time the sun was barely high enough in the sky to drive the dawn shadows away, Lieutenant Hanley was back. "Sergeant Saunders, a word with you, please." He pulled Saunders away from the squad position and said, "The Battalion S-2 says that kid Keeno is smart as paint. He wants to latch on to him for an interpreter. That okay with you? I kind of hate to let him go because Keeno wants to stay with us. We could use a gent like him ourselves. We'll be getting into Germany any day now. The more German-speakers we got the better. What do you think?"

Saunders tried to marshal his thoughts. What did he say now? It was one thing to banish Keeno for good, but it was quite another to let him go no farther than Battalion. If Keeno left the squad to stay at Battalion, the squad would never forgive Saunders. That would be a kind of treason they'd never understand. So Saunders stalled for time by lighting a cigarette, then said, "You don't think he's a security risk?" Briefly Saunders told the lieutenant of the trouble with Keeno and the attack the night before, finishing, ". . . so that's why I don't quite trust him."

But to Saunders' astonishment, Lieutenant Hanley just laughed. "He's only a kid, Sergeant. And a pretty scared one at that. He thinks you're about four cuts above the general, you know. I can't believe he's any kind of risk. For one thing, how could he communicate to the Germans? And the Battalion S-2 seems to trust him. He's the big Intelligence expert around here."

"Okay, sir. I'll tell you what we do. Let's compromise. I'll keep him in the squad, but I'll keep my eye on him in darned good style. The first time he gets the least bit out of line, bingo, he gets the ax. That okay?"

"Fair enough. I'll see he gets back to you."

Saunders made no attempt to explain things to the squad. He simply said his recommendations to Lieutenant Hanley had been overruled and Keeno was staying with the squad for the time being, to be carried as a squad supernumerary.

The cheer that announcement got from the squad was out of all proportion, Saunders thought, but there was no doubt everyone was happy. Keeno tackled the orderly and clean-up work with a violent enthusiasm, and for several days he was riding high. The battalion went into reserve for a time, and there was plenty of chance for Keeno to show what he could do in the way of KP, laundry, service, and general handiwork. But one morning things took a surprising turn. Saunders' misgivings piled up all over again.

The squad was billeted in a small barn, just a shack really, but it had a roof and they'd rigged makeshift tables, racks for the bedrolls, and in general were a lot more comfortable than they'd been for quite a while. The squad was falling out for some platoon training on the new smooth-surfaced grenades they were getting, and just as he moved the column out toward the range area, Saunders realized he'd forgotten his cigarettes. They were sitting on the egg-crate table in the middle of the squad room. Nelson was back there on charge-of-quarters duty to watch the weapons and gear, but was too far away to holler at. "Hey, Caje, take over." Saunders turned over the squad to Caje. "I'll be right back."

The sergeant trotted back into the billet, ducked through the door, and retrieved his cigarettes from the table before he realized that Nelson was nowhere in sight. Out back, maybe. Saunders glanced around the darkened room, and then a movement outside the makeshift window caught his eye. He walked over, glancing down. Saunders whistled silently at what he saw.

Below the window, on the strip of matted turf outside the shack, Keeno squatted, the walkie-talkie in one hand, a book of some sort in the other. Saunders' first impulse was to bellow at him, then to crawl Nelson, wherever he was, for letting this go on. But then, looking closer, he changed his mind. The book was a Field Manual on the walkie-talkie the kid was looking at. But why was he checking out the radio set? Wouldn't those things net with German radios if you adjusted them right?

Darned right they would.

So this was something to watch, to think about. Saunders shook his head as he walked back to rejoin the squad. Nothing would ever convince him that Keeno wasn't bad news for the squad. Nothing. Time, Saunders was certain, would show he was right. Keeno was a security risk. A kid spy.

4

"WE'RE AIRBORNE!"

Word came down by special runner to the platoon, typed on the misty carbon of a field-message blank: *All officers and non-commissioned officers of the first three grades assemble at Checkerboard Blue CP at 1400 hours today for important instructions. Signed, O'Connors, Major, S-3.*

Major O'Connors ran the meeting himself, a slender wiry man in one of those Armored Force zipper combat jackets that were warmer than the standard field jacket. His gold leaves were askew at his shoulders. He faced the group squatting on the slope outside the little cafe the battalion was using for a Command Post and after the adjutant checked the attendance, the major said, "I'll make this very quick because there's a lot

68

to get done." His voice crackled and a flicker of something like amusement moved in his hooded eyes. "The Old Man wanted you to get this straight from the beginning. Keeps the rumors down. So here's the word: Checkerboard Blue is attached to the 337th Glider Regiment of the 19th Airborne Division effective at once. Checkerboard Blue moves by truck at first light tomorrow and closes into the 337th area in the vicinity of Rheims just after noon. We'll get three-days special training, perhaps more, before we take part in certain classified operations you'll hear more about later. For now, alert your outfits for movement, stand by for the details of serials and march units, and—" here he paused and grinned, the smile smoothing the lines of his face, "don't anyone start counting that airborne pay yet. I don't know if we'll get it or not."

There was a murmur from the assembled officers and non-coms. Saunders felt the thin prickle of excitement wriggle along his spine. "Airborne! I think we must be going to shoot the wad!" he whispered to Lieutenant Hanley beside him.

And so they were. The company was billeted in a tent camp close to an airfield on the edge of Rheims, in sight of the famous cathedral spires. A sergeant from the glider regiment gave them their first orientation—K Company with Hanley's platoon and Saunders' squad assembled in front of strange-looking aircraft on the pierced-steel planking that made up most of the airfield.

"This here's an American glider, the CG4A," the sergeant said in a professional instructional tone. "It has no engine as you can all see, and it gets its motive power by being towed behind a C-47 aircraft, which is one of those big two-engine jobs you all saw down on the flight line near your tents. Now see how much we can get in one of these things. Okay, Kelly, boil outta there!"

Saunders looked at the glider, noticing that it was a single-wing job dark green in color, a good deal like the light planes the artillery used for observation except it had a blunt rounded nose and its small-wheeled landing gear was installed so close to the fuselage the glider sat barely a foot off the ground. It looked pretty much like it had been made of orange crates and salvage canvas and hardly seemed like it could get into the air, let alone carry troops and equipment.

But as Saunders watched, the rounded nose of the glider opened on a hinge at the top and the whole front end of the glider raised up much like a huge insect curling an upper lip. "Gee-ron-i-mo!" Led by a corporal Saunders took to be Kelly, an eight-man squad of infantry charged out of the glider in full combat gear. From the camouflage nets on their helmets to the baggy pants bloused over shiny jump boots they were ready to go.

With a professional eye, Saunders checked them off as they fell in in front of the glider. Weapons okay, including a BAR and a 60 milli-meter mortar; one, no two, rifles equipped with grenade launchers. Combat packs, extra ammo, K rations bulging huge side-pockets in the baggy pants, entrenching tools, walkie-talkie radio, flares, marking panels, everything was there.

Then, as if that weren't enough, at a word from the corporal two men dashed back inside the glider and shortly a loaded jeep rolled out, windshield battened down and covered, machine-gun pedestal mounted on the right running board, the rear well piled high with full barracks bags secured under a lashed tarp.

A ripple of amazement fluttered over the onlookers. "Hey, now, that's going to war in style." . . . "Get a load of the jeep, no more hikin' for us." . . . "Yeah, but how do you keep from falling through the bottom of that bucket?". . . "It gets you there but how does it get you home?"

"Not so fast, not so fast." The instructor held up both hands for silence. "In a minute you can all inspect the glider and check the equipment. But one thing you got to understand about the airborne. Some jump out of airplanes in parachutes and some go in by glider. But the whole purpose is to get us in deep against the enemy. We make a vertical envelopment, flying over the

enemy and dropping in behind him. We figure we can last for seventy-two hours on our own and by that time we have to get linked up with our ground tail. Somebody has to break through to us. The whole thing is, our job is only beginning when we get on the ground. We have to fight then just like you guys do. Only thing is, we're good and deep."

The sergeant paused, then said, "Just how deep you'll see when we get the word on the operation coming off. But that's not my department. You'll get orders on that. For now I want you to peel off by squads and just inspect the men and the equipment, ask any questions you want. When I blow the whistle, reassemble and we'll start instruction in loads and lashing, balance points, structure of the glider, in-flight techniques, unloading, and emergency procedures. Okay? Awright, squad leaders take charge of your squads and move out!"

"It is that emergency business I am suspicious of," Caje said to Saunders as they trotted over to look at the glider. "I think we could make a better glider by ourselves."

"Could be, Caje. But they used these things in Normandy and Holland already. They did okay."

"I do not like this airborne. If a man was supposed to have wings, he would have been born with them. Is it not so?"

"Relax, Caje. This is just an improvement on nature. The sergeant says these airborne outfits go deep. You wouldn't want to walk, would you?"

For answer, Caje shrugged, and gave his attention to testing the fabric of the glider with a bony finger. The thin material vibrated when he poked it, and Caje said, "You ever hear of antiaircraft fire, Sarge? This is one thing I will ask about."

Saunders grinned a reply and turned to examine the 60 millimeter mortar pack one of the demonstration squad was carrying. The 60 was a right handy little mortar. In Checkerboard Blue they were kept in the company weapons platoon and farmed out as required. Saunders wondered if each airborne squad got one; it would be a wonderful piece of fire support.

The rest of his squad thought so, too. "Of all the things we saw today," Nelson said when they were flaked out on the cots in the big tent waiting for evening chow, "I think I liked the idea of that jeep and the mortar best. We ride to war instead of walking. And when we get there we got a little heavy firepower."

"Don't bet we'll get it," Saunders growled. "I checked that out already. The lieutenant says we might or we might not. Depends on what our company mission is."

"Keeno can maybe scrounge us a mortar," Littlejohn said. "Best little scrounger I ever did see."

Saunders remained silent; Keeno was still a sore point with him and he said, "I've told you guys already. He can dog-rob all he wants to as long as the squad's stuck with him. But I don't want him fooling with equipment." Saunders was still thinking about the walkie-talkie and the fact he was convinced Keeno was a spy. "Where is he now, by the way?" he asked.

"I sent him to pick up the laundry from that French lady. He won't let us get overcharged," Kirby spoke up from where he was writing a letter on his bunk. "Speaking the lingo, he's got the Indian sign on all these people."

"I told him to get us some oil for the lantern from Supply." This from Nelson. "Be dark pretty soon. We got to have light in the tent when we black out for the night."

"He's supposed to be getting some more cleaning gear," Brockmeyer said. "The squad's weapon-cleaning-kit is low on patches, and besides, somebody glommed on to the extra cleaning rod."

"Great," Saunders said drily. "Everybody sent him off someplace, only nobody knows where he is. How do you know he's not out sabotaging the gliders right now? You heard what those guys said today about how important those control wires are. And what happened in England before D-Day."

Caje shook some dust from his black beret,

saying, "You are hard on the boy, Sergeant."

"The heck I am. I just want to know where he is."

The members of the squad exchanged glances and because Saunders was so conscious that his own view of Keeno was far apart from theirs he felt compelled by some perverse motivation to hammer the difference home, to exploit the gap he knew was widening among them on the subject of Keeno. "I'll tell you another thing," he said, his voice low and the words coming slowly and distinctly. "I'll admit I told you, Brock, to get the kid out of that sissy civilian smock and get him into some regular GI clothes. But you boobed it up."

Brock looked shocked. "Fouled it up? The kid's got a better pair of pants than I have."

"That's not what I'm talking about. I—" Saunders was spared the rest of the sentence because the tent flap parted and Keeno came in, the laundry, a big package wrapped in newspaper, in his arms.

"She jolly well did try to gaff us," Keeno said, dropping the package with a plop. He grinned quickly, and bounced happily across the tent. "One hundred francs for a dab of wash! I told her she'd ruddy well take ten, that's exactly what I did."

There was a murmur of approval from the squad as Keeno broke open the laundry and handed the clothing, clean, ironed, and smelling faintly of orris root, around. "Here's your drawers, Sergeant." Keeno extended Saunders' folded shorts. "All tickety-boo, I trust?"

Saunders took the shorts, dropped them on his bunk, and sat eyeing Keeno. "No, everything's not tickety-boo, whatever the heck that means." He took in the boy with a quick glance, from the knit woolen helmet undercap on his head to his field jacket a shade too big for him down to the OD pants stuffed into the combat boots. Then he moved his eyes back to the single stripe that gleamed on Keeno's jacket sleeve. The best way to finish the thought Keeno interrupted with his entrance was to take the action. But Saunders knew it would be an unpopular action and while that didn't bother him too much at this point, he wanted to be sure nobody missed it. "Who actually got you those clothes, Keeno? I told Brock to do it before we ever left your village area. But who actually gave them to you?"

Keeno looked at him, the white face drawn now, a shadow flitting across the dark eyes. The boy made a nervous gesture at his knit cap, as if he were going to take it off, then thought better of it. Suddenly he was a frightened pixie again. "I— I believe Doc, Sergeant, sir."

"Doc? *Doc!*" Saunders raised his voice to call the little medic who was outside the tent, putting chlorination pills in the Lister bag holding the drinking water in the company street. "Doc!"

When Doc, his helmet with the big red crosses looking too big for him, came in, he said, "You call, Sarge? What's up? Almost chow time, isn't it?"

"Never mind that for now." Saunders waited,

sensing the tension building up in the tent. The air held the peculiar harsh smell canvas tents always had. The cool crispness of the oncoming night outside carried the soft hubbub of the company falling in for chow. Saunders knew what he was about to do would hurt Keeno and hurt the squad. Nonetheless, he saw it as essential to his own hold on the squad, part of the larger task of keeping the firm unquestioned discipline the forthcoming operation would demand. So he hesitated a beat, until all eyes in the tent were on him, then said quietly, "Doc, where'd you get the kid's clothes?"

Doc looked at Saunders a long moment, his sensitive face shadowed under the big helmet. He toyed absently with the loose chin strap. Looking away he said, "You know where I got them, Sergeant."

"Maybe I do and maybe I don't. You tell me."

Doc raised his head suddenly, and there was an appeal in his eyes that was unmistakable. "It helped the squad, Sergeant. And the dead have to make way for the living, don't they?"

"I know you got those clothes off a dead man, Doc. And if I looked at the laundry marks I could probably tell you who it was. But that isn't what bothers me. It isn't that at all. It's how come you left the stripe on the sleeve. How come you did that?"

There was a sudden murmur from the others in the tent, but Saunders pressed the point. "You shouldn't have left the stripe on the sleeve, Doc. A private first-class is a soldier, Doc. A good one. And when he dies, the stripe goes to somebody who earns it. Not to some kid who needs a pair of pants. That clear?"

"It was the only jacket came even close to fitting him. I didn't even think about the stripe at all."

"Well, you should have. Civilians can't wear Army rank. It's bad enough they got to wear parts of the uniform." Saunders paused, looked once around at the squad, then said, "Keeno, take that stripe off. Right now. Got it?"

As if in a daze, Keeno looked at Saunders. His lower lip above the pointed chin trembled a little, and the dark eyes were huge in his white face. "Wh—whatever you say, Sergeant." Then he began plucking at the stripe with skinny fingers. "Whatever you say."

"Doggone it!" With a quick movement Kirby launched himself from the bed. With several fast strokes of his bayonet, he cut the stripes off Keeno's sleeves. Then Kirby jammed the bayonet into its scabbard with a *click!* He dropped the stripes in Saunders' lap. In a furious voice he said, "There you are, Sergeant. Does that satisfy you? Is everything okay by the book now, Sergeant? You bet it is!" Turning on his heel, Kirby caught up his mess gear and stormed out of the tent, flinging over his shoulder, "Come on, you guys, who's for chow?"

They all went out but Caje, who walked over to Keeno saying, "Go, boy. Get something to eat." Then as Keeno went out, Caje tossed his beret on his cot. Reaching down to pick up the cloth stripes, he twirled them between his broad thumb and finger. His dark eyes fixed Saunders. "You think that was necessary, Sergeant? The boy was very proud of these stripes."

"So was the soldier who wore them. The one that got killed fighting the Krauts."

"The squad did not mind. They wanted the boy to think he belonged."

Saunders came up off his bunk quickly, then stooped to pick up his mess gear. "That's the whole trouble. Can't they get it through their thick skulls this kid *doesn't* belong? Let me tell you something, Caje. You heard what they all said when I asked where Keeno was. Somebody sent him for the laundry. Somebody else sent him for oil. Somebody on top of that had him after cleaning gear. The whole squad takes this kid for granted because he does all the dirty work. Is that any way to do? Well, is it?"

When Caje didn't answer but just stood there, looking at the stripes twirling slowly in his fingers, Saunders said, "Okay, the heck with it. I'm going

to chow." And as he left the tent, Saunders muttered, not caring whether anyone was there to
hear him or not, "Who are we anyway, to have a
dog-robber? He's nothing but trouble. With a
capital T."

5

"A CLEVER FORM OF MUTINY. . . ."

Saunders drove the squad hard over the next few days.

There were a number of reasons, he kept telling himself. The big one, of course, was the operation. They were going into Germany by glider, part of a corps-sized airborne operation set up to wrestle a toehold on the Rhine. Nobody knew exactly where or when yet, but that's what they were going to do. Shoot the wad and go for the Rhine. In a way, it was a compliment to Checkerboard Blue to be a part of it. And the squad wasn't going to goof up its mission, whatever it turned out to be.

Next, a lot of this was a new deal. The airborne had a whole new technique K Company and the squad had to learn. Vertical envelopment they called it, and it was like a high-looping hook thrown at the enemy's jaw. *The Stars & Stripes* newspaper kept telling how American troops were edging into Germany now that the Allies were attacking the Siegfried Line again, but this airborne deal was going to go deep. Clear to the Rhine River which was so important to the war. That meant you had to learn loading and everything else from how they figured the chalk numbers on the glider noses to tell you which one was yours down to why gliders had a center of gravity and special tie-down points for the loads. Communications, supply, fire support, everything was a little different because the airborne was a different outfit. You fought like infantry when you got down on the ground, but the tricky part was getting there. Airborne troops were as vulnerable as a wet paper sack that first couple of hours after they landed. All the power of men, weapons, artillery, and combat know-how got scattered by parachute drop and glider landing. You had to organize quick, form up, reshape yourself, while all the time maybe the Germans were counterattacking you.

Counterattack! That was what they sweated most. If you were fragmented and couldn't get collected, even a Kraut outfit of regimental size could give you fits, no matter if you were an airborne division four or five times as big. If you got scattered by high ground winds, or failed to hit the DZs as they called the Drop Zones, if too many gliders cracked up when they went sailing in, well, that's all there would be. You lost your combat effectiveness. A counterattack could wipe you up in nothing flat.

That was why security was so important. That's why nobody knew where they were going yet. Because if the Krauts even got an inkling that an airborne operation was underway, they could reorganize their Rhine defenses, rearrange their troops in the flat plains along the Rhine. They'd put in anti-airborne defenses by the mile— sharpened stakes, log barriers, wire nets—any- thing to impale a paratrooper or to flip a glider on its back. They'd be sitting there ready for you.

Loaded and locked. Ready for you.

So Saunders drove the squad hard. He spared nobody. "Caje, you did this tie-down!" Saunders kicked a taut lashing and watched it snap loose. "You want that jeep rolling into your lap when we take off?"

"Doc, look at that pack." Saunders flashed a hand at the poorly fastened flap on the medical kit. "You want those bandages falling out of the glider from a thousand feet?"

"You, Littlejohn. You keep that BAR right next to me. You got to move faster when we clear the glider in the DZ. You got to move, man. *Move!*"

But there was another reason, unstated, unspecified, nonetheless there. Saunders knew it, the squad knew it, and it hung among them like a heavy burden no one was willing to carry because you shrank from the responsibility.

Keeno.

The kid himself hadn't changed. He went about his many tasks as eagerly and as cheerfully as before, Saunders had to give him that. But ever since that night in the tent when Saunders made him take the Pfc stripes off his sleeves, the squad sided with Keeno against Saunders. Nothing you could put your finger on, of course, but Saunders was perceptive enough, knew his men well enough, so that he could sense their attitude as easily as he could call the men by name.

Take the matter of the 60 millimeter mortar. They were issued a mortar but got no extra man to handle it, and they likewise had an attached jeep with driver. They were shaping up like the demonstration squad they'd seen their first day, though it turned out the jeep didn't really belong to the squad. It was one of the company jeeps and just traveled in their glider until it got on the ground. Then it reverted to the control of the company commander. But the mortar was theirs, a little piece of plumbing that looked to be little more than a section of gas pipe sitting on a metal plate, but it could lob an HE (high explosive) shell an incredible distance. It made a fine complement to the flat-trajectory fire of the BAR, not only because it packed more wallop with its HE shell, but because it made very little noise when it went off. You fired it by pulling the arming wire off a pear-shaped shell hardly bigger in your hand than a baseball, then dropped the round, tailfirst down the pipe. It went off when the firing pin inside the base of the tube actuated the primer. *Koff!* With a little puppylike bark the shell went hurtling through the air. You could almost follow it with your eye. *Whammmm!* It detonated anywhere up to a good mile in front of you. The Krauts couldn't hear it coming either. Mortar shells, traveling slower than artillery rounds and falling in from a high angle, made no whistle. First thing you knew, they were bursting right on top of you. If the Krauts hated mortar fire even half as much as the Americans did, the squad was big money ahead with a sixty.

So Saunders insisted everyone get checked out on the mortar. You never knew what casualties you might have, and this was only prudence.

Everybody should be able to sight it and shoot it. So he asked Kirby, "What'd you do with the baseplate, Kirby? I want to take a little time after chow for some mortar drill."

"Keeno's got it, Sarge. He's checking the alignment."

"*Keeno's* got it?" Saunders made no attempt to conceal his anger. Keeno was tinkering with the mortar now, was he? For a blind moment Saunders' temper seethed and boiled, then he got control of himself. Instead of popping off, he said, "Kirby, assemble the squad. Keeno included. And do it now. Got it? Okay. Move out."

That the squad was a little slow in assembling in the tent was itself a mark of the way the Keeno situation had gotten out of hand. Obviously Kirby had told them all the sergeant was teed off again, this time about something to do with Keeno and the mortar. They dragged into the tent like unwilling schoolboys being hauled before a teacher, a fact that didn't improve either the squad's or Saunders' disposition any. When the last man—Littlejohn again—slumped down onto a bunk in the tent, Saunders moved to the center-pole, leaned against it casually, and said, "Okay, you guys, now get this. I've called you together to get this Keeno business out in the open once and for all. Now what did I tell you just the other day about Keeno and the equipment?"

Not waiting for an answer Saunders went on, "Since obviously none of you were paying any attention at the time, I'll tell you what I said. I said I didn't want him fooling with the equipment. I meant it or I wouldn't have said it. So the latest is he's tinkering with the mortar base-plate. Now let me tell you something. That mortar's one of our best friends. It may save our lives in this Donnybrook whenever it comes off. That's why I got you all sweating over it. But it isn't—you say something, Keeno?"

"Yes, Sergeant," the boy spoke up this time in a firm voice. "The carrying-handle in the base-plate was. . . ."

"Never mind that." Saunders cut him off.

"Anything wrong we can't fix in the squad, we take it to the company armorer. That's what he's for." Then he went on. "It's not the mortar base-plate I'm sounding off about. It's what it represents. Here's a vital piece of equipment that needs attention and when it doesn't need attention it needs all the tender loving care we can give it. Right?"

Nobody argued with that so Saunders went on. "I'll tell you what's happening in this squad and if you think about it, you'll admit it. I'll bet some of you feel this way already, deep-down. So let me tell you. We're no better than the Krauts and their slave laborers. No, let me finish, darn it. Don't interrupt. It's the home-cooked truth, and here's why. You guys haven't done anything more with Keeno than to make him a military flunky who does all the work you should be doing. That's exactly right. And I can prove it. Who's supposed to take care of the mortar today? Kirby. Who carries the squad cleaning kit? Littlejohn. Who sent him for lantern oil when he was CQ and should have gone himself? Nelson. Who stuck up

for him when I took a soldier's rank off him? Caje
and the rest of you. But who did all the work?
Keeno, that's who."

Saunders looked around him, a wry expression
twisting his mouth and his voice harsher now.
"You've got yourselves so wound up in this kid
and what you think he can do that you're no better
than the Germans who've got his old man in a
slave-labor camp right now! You—"

"Aw, Sarge." . . . "Hey, now!" . . . "Easy with
the whip, for gosh sake!" . . . "What kind of talk
is that?"

Saunders stopped the chorus of squawks by
raising his hands. But Caje spoke before Saunders
could.

"Sergeant!" Caje's black eyes snapped and the
long slope of his face was suddenly stiff. "You
cannot say thees!" As always when he was angry,
Caje's accent was heavier than usual. "You cannot put us in a class with the *Boche!* Wha' you
mean, Sergeant?" Caje took a slow step toward
Saunders, hands hooking a little at the level of

his belt. "Wha' you mean, Sergeant, saying thees?"

Saunders took a step forward himself. This was the whole trouble, of course. At a time when squad unity counted for everything, when they had to pull together better than ever before, they were splitting out. All because of the kid, Keeno. "You think I'm all wet, don't you? But there's none of you dares ask himself any questions too hard." Saunders paused, and let his mouth curl. "That goes for you, Caje, and everybody else. What are you guys giving up for all this service, anyway? Not a solitary thing. I haven't heard anyone mention paying him, have I? You're darned tootin' I haven't. I—"

"It's not brass I'm seeking, Sergeant." Keeno spoke up quietly, taking a step nearer Caje. "It's a chance to serve."

Saunders stepped back, tossing his hands in a negligent gesture. "Sure, a chance to serve," he said sarcastically. "To serve who? Adolf Hitler?"

"*Enough!*" Caje bellowed the word, and

turned to face the squad. Suddenly he changed his tone, but the harsh lines grooving his face showed the strain he was under. "It is time to speak openly. You are accusing the squad of a selfishness, of a disregard, of a meanness against this boy, is it not so, Sergeant?"

"You got it."

"You yourself do not trust Keeno. You think he is a danger and a security risk?"

"You're reading me loud and clear."

"Very well. We are at your orders. What are your wishes?"

Saunders hesitated. Knowing Caje as he did, this wasn't like the big bayou jumper. He'd backed down too quickly; now he was dangerously quiet. And like the cottonmouths of his native Louisiana, a quiet Caje wound tight as a dollar watch was a man to look out for. So Saunders fenced for a moment, not sure exactly why. "What do you want to hear, orders or wishes?"

"Orders. For certain."

Saunders took a deep breath. This was the time

to face up to the whole mess, to break it off once and for all and then concentrate on pulling the squad together into the kind of team they had to be if they were all going to walk away from the airborne operation coming up. "Okay, I'll tell you what my orders are. I want Keeno out of here by suppertime tomorrow night. And that doesn't mean just turning him loose down the road. I want him in the custody of the Division Chaplain, the Civil Affairs officer, or some other responsible party. That way we'll know he's in good hands. But they won't be ours."

Caje laughed, a rousing bellow that stabbed the silence of the tent like a dirk. Then he slapped Keeno lightly on the shoulder. "Speak your piece, boy. Tell the Sergeant what arrives."

Keeno took a deep breath, and looking very carefully at Saunders out of his deep lambent eyes, he said, "I'm that ashamed, Sergeant, being such a burden to you. But the heart of the matter is, the squad thought I might be after meeting up with my da. They've promised to help. Do I go to the parson's, this plan will never come through. I'll be that much farther out of things, do you see? And certainly"—Keeno paused and swallowed— "even you do not wish me that much ill."

Saunders gritted his teeth. This was why Caje had acted the way he did. Pretty slick, too. He got Saunders to commit himself, then sprung this as the topper. Now it made Saunders look a bigger heel than ever if he broke this particular arrow. In a way, it was a clever form of mutiny—nothing you could put your finger on, but Caje had put Saunders clearly in the position of being the villain of the piece. The change in roles was subtly done, and that's what made it tough. Before the squad unity hung on Saunders' ability to establish his own ascendancy from a position of basic strength as squad leader. Now Caje's gambit put him way back in the bushes as the guy doing the dirty work. It was a long way back out. So Saunders began by fencing a little, doing a little exploring, the way a good soldier begins any battle. "So you're going to meet your da, are you, Keeno?

Last I knew, your father was somewhere around Wesel. Just how did the squad propose getting you there?"

Nobody said anything for a minute, then Brockmeyer spoke up, his stolid Dutch face impassive, his voice heavy. "All the rumors say that's where we're dropping, Sarge. So we put the kid in a glider and fly him in."

Saunders thrust both hands into his back pockets, turned and took three long steps toward the rear of the tent, then turned again and came forward into the center. "Oh, the rumors are saying we're going to Wesel, are they? That makes it gospel, does it? That becomes the basis of defying my orders with some half-masted plan to smuggle this kid into Germany, does it?" Saunders shook his head in dismay. "I've heard some beauts in my time, but this one takes the rag off'n the bush." Suddenly he jabbed a finger at the group. "Now get this, you clowns, and get it right and get it straight. If the rumors say we're going to Wesel, it's because the Division wants the word passed we're going to Wesel. Did you ever hear of a deception plan? So it's nothing to build any hopes on, let alone make commitments you can't keep to a kid, just to salve your own dirty consciences. Next, even if we were going to Chalons-sur-Marne which must be all of three kilometers from here, I wouldn't let you take that kid in by glider if he bought a fistful of tickets. Security, deception, everything else aside, I wouldn't let it happen because that isn't how Chip Saunders runs his squad." He wet his lips quickly, ran a hand through his tousled hair, then went on. "So don't try to back me in a corner by giving me this youse-is-a-viper routine because you think you're going to put the kid somewhere near his old man. You forget it. Once and for all. Is that clear?"

Nobody said anything. For a long moment Saunders looked around the squad, hard eyes traveling from face to face. "Caje? Kirby? Little-john? You got it? You better believe it you have. What about you, Brock? Nelson? Doc? You roger for the message? Yeah, darn right you do, five by five." Then turning: "And how about you, Keeno? You got it?"

Keeno didn't say anything. He looked at Saunders with his dark eyes unreadable in his pointed little face and then, without saying a word, turned away, reached under a cot, and pulled out his little briefcase. Then as slowly as if he was wading through molasses, not looking at anyone, he went silently out of the tent.

6

"IT'S MY SQUAD!"

Behind Keeno, as the flap closed after him, a pool of silence seemed to swirl inside the tent, threatening to engulf Saunders. For a long moment he stood there, thinking that no matter how much you might learn in a war about shooting and killing, you never learned all there was to know about people. Never.

Clearly, the mood of the squad was changing now, as if Keeno's going had put a period to one phase of an operation and kicked off another one. The belligerency washed out of the faces around Saunders in a sort of group double-take, as if individually and collectively the squad was taking a good hard look at itself. Caje twisted his black beret in his big hands; Kirby's mouth was open, eyes staring; Nelson's jaw was pulled down and Brock and Littlejohn looked shocked. Saunders said quietly, "Doc. Follow him. If he tries to go very far get him by the ear and deliver him to the Division Chaplain."

Then, as Doc went out, Caje spoke up, the words coming slow. "Sarge, I should have thought it all out. I was wrong. You are right. We have not done well by the boy. It is so. We have been selfish. Very selfish."

"Yeah," Kirby said. "We thought we had it made in the shade. We never thought how Keeno might be taking it."

"You said a full mouth, Kirby boy." This from Littlejohn. "I told you guys you shouldn'ta done it."

"Okay, everybody," Saunders said quietly. "Knock it off." He didn't trust himself to say much more. Because he'd misread the squad reaction after all. It was plain that nobody saw it from Saunders' own view yet. All at once Keeno was an object of pity to the squad, and so in some ways was more of a liability than if he were being merely exploited. When you pity someone for a while, he becomes a burden. Saunders knew that very well. And they had enough burdens as it was. And then, because it was still Keeno who had created this situation, who was responsible for the split in the squad and the turn events were taking, Saunders lashed out at him again, not caring that in its present mood the squad would see this only as a needless cruelty. "Let the little schnook go. It makes it easier on everybody. One less freeloader is okay by me." In some perverse way, Saunders felt glad at the turn of events. It was fitting reward for a spy. So he flung one last phrase. "I don't like spies, no matter how small they are."

Then Saunders stalked from the tent, intending to find a quiet spot to write a long-overdue letter to his folks, but the platoon runner found him before he got started. "Lieutenant wants you right away, Sarge. On the double."

Saunders found Lieutenant Hanley in a musty room in the sagging barracks the company was using for a headquarters and officers' billet. Hanley was seated on his cot in his OD undershirt. Next to the single window, staring at the floor, Keeno sat very stiffly on the edge of a rickety chair.

"What's the latest wheeze on the boy here, Saunders?" Lieutenant Hanley asked the question briskly. "The security patrol picked him up trying to get over the fence. He says you ran him off. That right?"

Saunders looked at Keeno, sitting primly against the windowsill, his briefcase clutched at his knees. His black hair was awry under his knit cap, the dark eyes were shadowed with sadness, and there was a forlorn twist to his mouth. Saunders felt a sudden twinge of sympathy for the boy—he looked about as helpless as a wet puppy on ice—but he pushed the thought away. After all, there was evidence of the ammunition case, the walkie-talkie, and now the mortar. You had to go by the facts. So he said, "Maybe run him off's a hard way to put it. But I did issue orders to get him into the hands of the Division Chaplain by tomorrow night."

Hanley raised his eyebrows. "You got the word then? The captain tell you?"

"Word? I don't get you."

"You said 'tomorrow night.' "

"Sure I did. But I knew it would take about that long to get him to Division headquarters. That's all."

"Oh." The lieutenant paused, started to say something, then paused again. "I'll come back to that later," he went on. He indicated Keeno with a nod. "You really got it in for the boy, Saunders? I think maybe you're being a little rough on him, from what little I've heard around. I can't get the boy to tell me a thing. Fill me in, will you?"

Saunders gave him a rundown on the events in the tent and the story on removing the Pfc stripe, finishing, "Maybe I haven't explained it very well, but you'll have to believe me, Lieutenant. I know that squad like I know the inside of my hat. And our teamwork is suffering. The squad unity is breaking down. All on account of this kid, here."

"Sounds to me like the squad doesn't know how to handle this situation. Maybe they never had it so good, all this dog-robber business. What about you, Keeno? How do you feel about all this?"

Keeno fixed the lieutenant with those big eyes, then said in a small voice, "Sergeant Saunders is our NCO, sir. I am subject to his orders. He wants me to leave. So I nipped out of there, sir. I—I'll not be after making trouble, sir."

Lieutenant Hanley tugged at his undershirt at his beltline, looking as if he'd never seen it before. Then he fixed Saunders with a hard glance, and blinking, said, "You sure you aren't overdoing all this?"

"Could be. But I don't think so."

The lieutenant shook his head. "Well, I'm not so sure. Seems to me maybe you are overdoing it. It's been a long war. Lot of people got hurt." He looked at Keeno. "Not all of them soldiers either." Then abruptly, he said, "Where's your mother, Keeno? Where do you think?"

"I—I've no idea, sir. That—that's why I was so charged up at getting into Germany. If I could find my da, we could find my mother."

Lieutenant Hanley cocked his head. "A pretty long shot. And sometimes the long shots pay off. But you couldn't go in with a glider. The sergeant's right about that. It'll have to be some other way. Got any ideas, Saunders?"

Startled, Saunders said, "Ideas? Not me. I just want him out of the squad."

Lieutenant Hanley stood up. "Here's what we're going to do. We'll compromise. Saunders, I want you to knock off giving this boy a hard time. I want—"

"Sir, may I make a comment?" Saunders interrupted the lieutenant. He was stung by the lieutenant's remark. Sensing that the basic issue of his own control over the squad was being lost in the wave of the lieutenant's sympathy, Saunders went ahead quickly. "I'm not giving him a hard time.

I'm just interested in military efficiency."

"Nobody's denying that," the lieutenant said in a patient tone. "I know why you're doing this. You want to maintain the squad at peak combat efficiency. But look at this boy for a minute. Forget the security risk business, all that stuff. Here's a youngster that's taken his own kind of pasting from the war. Can't you see he's got to sort of get a new grip on things himself? Why isn't it just as important to help him fight his battle as it is to fight the Krauts? We're still human beings, aren't we, Saunders? We're not just killing-machines, are we?"

"I—I don't know, Lieutenant. I guess you're right." Saunders didn't quite know what to say. He could see what the lieutenant was getting at, he wasn't that dense. But there was a question of priority here, wasn't there? Which were you going to fight first? The battle with the Krauts or the battle in the backwash of war? Or was it all the same thing? How could you tell? "Okay, Lieutenant," Saunders said wearily. "I'll admit maybe

I've been rough on him. That's because with me the squad comes first. Maybe I resent an intruder, even if he is only a kid."

"I know your squad comes first. That's right and proper. You wouldn't be a good squad leader otherwise. But you have a heart, too, Saunders. And nobody knows it better than I do."

Saunders grinned quickly, anxious to clear the air. "I'll remind you of that heart business next time I ask you for a three-day pass, Lieutenant." Then he set his jaw. "But there's a big problem of military efficiency here. I think the squad is down over this whole thing. No question about it. I can't see taking the boy back there. What I suggest is this, Lieutenant."

"You suggest what? I'm listening."

"Keeno's got to get squared away, I'll admit that all right. So let's put him in the hands of the refugee control people instead of the Chaplain. The Civil Affairs Officer here ought to be able to help him more than anyone else. They do all the business with the civilians, right?" Because he saw a good solution at no cost to the squad or to his own position as the squad leader, Saunders warmed to the proposal. "They can even get him in touch with the Red Cross or maybe some French outfit that can track his mother down. I think that's the most practical approach. She may even be back in his own village. They couldn't have evacuated too far. They were all on foot."

"What do you think of that, Keeno?" Lieutenant Hanley reached out a hand and rubbed the knit cap on Keeno's head. "That way you won't have to go to war with the squad or anything."

"But I want to go to war with the squad! It's my squad. I belong there! I—"

"Hey now!"

"Slow down!"

Startled by Keeno's sudden outburst, Lieutenant Hanley and Sergeant Saunders both spoke at once. Saunders, surprised, nonetheless found he could understand Keeno's attitude and he begrudgingly admitted he respected him for it. But a young kid was a drag, a burden; he'd already

made up his mind about all that. So he said quietly, "Never mind, Keeno. You won't miss much.
Just a lot of mud and wet and being scared twenty-
four hours a day. You haven't seen much of that
yet, but that's all it is. Right, Lieutenant?"

Lieutenant Hanley was shrugging into his shirt
now and he seemed to pick up Saunders' cue because he spoke with a forced cheerfulness. "You
bet that's right. Why, I'd like to be going to refugee control myself. I'd get out of all the trouble
that's waiting for me." He buttoned up his shirt
and put on his field jacket, then reached out and
gently seized Keeno's briefcase. "Come on,
young feller. Let's go for a little jeep ride." Then
to Saunders he said, "Go on and go back. I'll get
him to the Civil Affairs people right now." Then
he winked. "I'll check with you later. Couple of
things to talk about."

Keeno looked wildly around, as if he were going to make a quick break, then sagged against
the window. "Whatever we do," he said in a tired
voice, "we have to have military efficiency, don't

we?" Then he moved toward the door as Lieutenant Hanley went out.

Saunders, trailing after them, found himself thinking, *He's a gutsy little apple, I'll give him that. Wanted to stay with the squad in spite of everything.* But then he checked himself. You couldn't get emotional about things. And even if you forgot all the security business, there was still the question of military efficiency. You just couldn't fight a war with kids. It was as simple as that. Whistling, Saunders headed back to the squad.

But no matter how loud he whistled, no matter how many trills and tones he managed, the picture stayed in his mind: A skinny figure in GI clothing a little too big for him, wool-knit cap perched on the black hair, pointed jaw set, and black eyes beseeching, ". . . It's my squad! I belong there!"

Now how about that? How *about* that?

Saunders shook his head to dismiss the picture from his mind. One of the things he'd learned thus far in the war was not to give way to his emotions. You couldn't afford it; it was a luxury a soldier couldn't allow himself. Because none of them could look forward to anything but more of the same they'd had so far—day after day and night after night of going down the road the hard way. Fire and maneuver, fire and go forward, fire and fall back, but always keep firing. Kill or be killed.

That was the doughfoot's lot in the war, and the only way you were going to get the war over with was to concentrate on the killing. Doing that didn't leave much left for anything else, and the softer emotions like compassion, sympathy, and a human understanding of your fellowman had to give way to the baser instincts that let you get the first shot in before somebody else shot you. That took every bit of energy and juice you could bring to it.

More, if you got interested in somebody, worried about him, made him a big buddy, well, the chance was better than even that he'd get his one of these days, and where were you? Saunders shook his head again. Nobody knew any better than he did that a little bit of you died when one of your men got hurt.

The trick was to keep that little bit that did the dying as small as possible. You couldn't do your job if you got too close to your men. So he'd done the right thing in this Keeno deal. Out of sight, out of mind. . . .

Lieutenant Hanley, when he showed up at the squad tent, called Saunders out to the jeep. "I got the boy squared away," he said. "Civil Affairs knows how to handle refugees. You can forget about him. But I wanted to tell you, you startled me a little when you came up with the 'tomorrow night' business. I was told to keep it all quiet so's nobody gets the word too soon, but I'll tell you. Don't tell the squad yet. But when we go down to the practice flights tomorrow they're going to seal us in." Then he grinned. "We're going to get our mission!"

"You sure?" Saunders couldn't share the lieutenant's enthusiasm. "We hardly got acquainted with those gliders, seems to me. I'm not sure we're ready."

The lieutenant shook his head. "You know what Napoleon said: 'Ask anything of me but time.' That's our big problem. Time. If this thing waits too long, a vertical envelopment won't do any good. The Krauts'll be ready for us. We have to go quick."

Saunders nodded, then said, "Let me ask you one thing. You satisfied with the way things are going? You think we can cut this airborne racket? I have a few doubts myself. We really could use more time."

Lieutenant Hanley gripped Saunders' arm for a brief moment, then dropped his hand. "Yeah, I'm satisfied." He fixed Saunders with a searching glance. "And I'll tell you one thing, Chip Saunders. If I have to go to war, whether I walk in these old boots or whether I fly in one of these paper-and-string glider jobs, there's nobody I'd rather go with than you." He grinned quickly, as if to disguise the compliment a little. "You and that raunchy squad of yours." He directed the jeep back into the road. "Okay, soldier. See you in the loading area tomorrow. Don't forget to take your airsick pills."

As the jeep headed back toward headquarters, Saunders stared after the lieutenant for a long moment, then turned and went into the tent. He had a nice warm feeling in his chest, but there was a little wriggle of worry just behind his belt buckle, too. It had to do with that raunchy squad. What kind of team were they really going to be now? Was the Keeno business really over and done with? Or wasn't it? Can the squad really cut the buck on its new mission, whatever it is?

7

"WHAT'S THIS WAR ABOUT?"

The squad was different now. No question about it.

Saunders thought the practice flights went well enough; they'd passed the loading inspection without a gig, bucked and lurched aloft behind the C-47 tow-plane for an hour and a half, nobody sick this time, hit their drop zone on the head, made the platoon rendezvous on schedule, and otherwise done a good workmanlike job. But the fire was gone.

Sitting in the cab of the big deuce-and-a-half truck that was taking the platoon back to camp at the end of the day Saunders didn't waste any time wondering why they hadn't been sealed in for their mission as Lieutenant Hanley had predicted. Things never happened the way they were supposed to in the Army. In due time they'd get their mission and get back in the shooting war again. No need to hurry it. Rather, he gave himself over to reviewing the events of the day, trying to put his finger on the exact nature of the problem. The main issue was plain, of course. The squad was teed off about Keeno.

Saunders took off his helmet, put it in his lap, and ran a hand through his tousled hair. He had to take that main issue apart to see where each man fit into it, and somehow, by his own personal leadership, get each guy back in step with the squad. But what was the best way to do it? It wasn't the kind of thing you could talk over with each man, hold his hand, pat him on the head, and say everything was over and done with. Doing that meant you put yourself in the hands of your subordinates, and when the time came to give the hard order, when the time came to say, "Charge that hill," or, "Clear that ditch," well, the old moxie would be gone. So a good leader didn't put himself in the hands of his men. He acted as he thought best. All the time.

Saunders shook his head. This was a rough one. You didn't find any answers in the book. You just drew on your own experience, your perception, and the intuitions that had been sharpened by the several months of banging across France with these jokers. The thing to do, it looked like, was to keep them headed into the main stream of squad activity and then play it by ear, hoping that somehow you could get everything pulled up right before the shooting started again.

The opportunity came sooner than Saunders expected. "What's this exercise?" Saunders asked the question as he came back into the tent after evening chow to find most of the squad crouching in various attitudes, almost every man burrowing through his barracks bag. "Well, sound off, somebody. What's up?"

Caje spoke first, straightening up at his bunk, his lean-jawed face solemn. "We have the word the boy Keeno goes to the refugee center tomorrow. He doesn't have too much, Sergeant."

"So? You still didn't answer my question."

Caje turned away. "We were thinking we could send him a few things. To help out." Caje tossed a knitted sweater onto the blanket in the middle of the tent floor. "You are welcome to join or not. Suit yourself."

Saunders looked at the sweater where it plopped on the blanket. "That's the sweater your sister sent you, isn't it, Caje?"

Caje avoided a direct answer. "I don't need it anymore."

Saunders walked over to his bunk, put his mess gear back in his pack, then sat down on his cot. Caje treasured that sweater, no question about it. It was a thick turtleneck done in GI-colored yarn and it could keep a lot of cold out. "You think spring is here, that it, Caje?"

"Sometimes it takes more than a sweater to keep a man warm, Sergeant."

There was no good answer to that, so Saunders, playing it light, said to Nelson, "Why don't you give the kid another case of ammunition?

Maybe he'll join the Resistance with it."

Nelson, squatting, looked up. "Very funny, Sergeant. Very funny. You ever think what it's like to be all by yourself, no home, no folks, no nothin'? That boy ain't old enough to handle something like that." Nelson found what he was looking for and tossed it onto the blanket.

Saunders' eyebrows went up. It was a wad of money, quite a bit, too. Nelson had been saving it since the beach for the pass he hoped to get in Paris someday. "No singing and dancing and ha-ha-ha in Paree now, hey, Nelson?"

"So who needs it?"

There was a sullen atmosphere in the tent now, as if the squad had somehow closed ranks against Saunders, excluding him from this activity as a not-too-subtle punishment for his part in disposing of Keeno. Saunders knew he had to be careful not to charge this invisible barrier too hard. If he did, he'd only bounce off it and be farther out of the picture than before. There was a sudden tightness in his chest, telling him that this bothered him more than he might have suspected. At the same time, he knew that he had to jelly along with it for the time being, let it work itself out. So he said to Littlejohn, "What about you, country boy? Anything you got is too big for the kid. He could sleep in one of your shoes."

"Mebbe so, Sergeant. But this'll take care of him while he's in the sack, wherever he finds one." With a quick flip of his hand Littlejohn tossed his Saint's medal onto the blanket, watching it almost yearningly as it rolled into one of the folds in Caje's sweater.

Well now, Saunders thought, *that's something, isn't it?* Of all the men in the squad, Saunders knew better than anyone else how much that medal meant to Littlejohn. It was his protection, his shield, and it was a fair statement to say he'd rather give his right arm away than that little medal. The act itself was the best measure so far of how the squad felt. Saunders wondered if he hadn't really missed the boat on this drill. These guys were really taking this big.

"What's with you, Doc? You going to send him a couple cans of foot powder?"

Doc turned his head from where he crouched at his first-aid packs. Doc was maybe the deepest one in the squad. Perhaps more than anyone else, Saunders knew, Doc had the gift of sympathy and understanding. Saunders, on his own part, was glad he didn't have this gift himself; it would have made being squad leader too tough. But he could respect and admire the quality in Doc. It made him a better medic and a better man. Saunders repeated the question. "No foot powder?"

"I'll tell you what I think he ought to get, Sergeant. Something I believe he'd treasure more than anything else." Doc stood up, a little man with a youthful face, the barely formed planes of his jaw shadowed now by some deep pain in his eyes. "But I suppose he'll never get it."

"What are you talking about?"

"A few kind words from you, Sergeant. You ought to know better than anyone else that a man can put up with a lot if he thinks his buddies are pulling for him. And young Keeno really thinks he belongs to this squad. He knows we all believe that. Every one of us. Except you."

"Except me. That's right."

"So why don't you break down? Send the kid a note or something? Send him a couple of candy bars, anything to let him know you aren't down on him."

Saunders shook his head. "Because I don't operate that way. I've already spoken my piece, both around here and with the lieutenant. Keeno has got all the fix on me that he's ever going to get."

Doc turned away. "Suit yourself, Sergeant. But a little warmth and understanding would go farther with that kid than all the supplies and equipment in this whole camp."

"Okay, Brockmeyer!" Saunders raised his voice a notch. "What are you mumbling about over there? Say it where I can hear it."

Brockmeyer's stolid face didn't change expression. He tossed some chocolate bars, squashed a little by long tenure in his barracks bag, onto the blanket. "All I said was, Sergeant, that when they issued you they left the warmth and understanding right on the Supply Room shelf."

That hurt. Saunders felt the jab deep within his ribs, but he knew better than to lash back. Because this was a situation you couldn't wrestle to a fall by sheer physical effort. You had to let it all shape itself up and then deal with it in terms of intangibles you could muster from within yourself, like leadership, personality, character, and weight of logic. It was nothing you could handle by direct attack. So Saunders let Brockmeyer's barb ride, merely saying, "You'll get him in bad habits with all those bars. He'll trade them on the black market."

"Could be," Brockmeyer said, "but it'll let him know we're thinking about him. And that's the whole idea."

With the same intuitive lift he always felt when he saw the solution to a combat problem, Saunders thought Brockmeyer's answer might be the handle to swing this thing with, but he wanted to do a little more probing, so he said, "What are you rooting for in there, Kirby? You started this whole thing. Maybe we ought to just send you."

Kirby whirled from bending over his barracks bag, eyes snapping, and the words tumbling. "Maybe you should, doggone it, maybe you should! All I wanted to do was help the squad and help you. And I wanted to help the kid, too. Ask any of the guys!" Kirby paused, took a deep breath, and then spoke in a calmer tone. "What's this war all about anyway, Sarge? You think you got all the answers just because we got this far? Sure, we knocked off our share of Krauts, we're professional killers all right. But ya know something? Being a professional killer in this war means you're a professional at staying alive so you got to have something to stay alive for!"

"Nobody said you didn't, Kirby. Least of all me."

"Aw, that's not what I'm talking about. You think we like all this stuff? You think we like walking over half of Europe with our guts in knots, wondering when we're going to get it, killing a bunch of guys so we won't?"

"It's them or you, Kirby. It's as simple as that."

"I know that! But that doesn't make it *right*. And that doesn't mean you can't worry about the little people in this war, does it?"

"No, it doesn't. But you have to keep that in perspective." Saunders thought he could see the handle in good focus now. He thought he knew the tack to take, and so he moved into the idea quickly. "That's the trouble with this outfit. You lost your perspective. The whole darned squad."

"What do you mean?" Two or three asked the question at once. "What do you mean, we lost our perspective?"

"You can't see the woods an account of the trees, that's what I mean. And now that you guys laid some of this stuff out where I can get at it, I'll explain this a little farther. You know what Keeno really is? He's a symbol to you blokes, that's all. He's a focus for the better nature of every man here in the squad, someone handy at a time when maybe you need something like that to convince yourselves you're still men and human beings after all. You maybe don't recognize that, but there's proof right there on that blanket. Practically everybody's given something he really treasures, trying to give a part of himself. Isn't that right?"

There was a moment of silence, then Doc said, "I think we all knew that, Sarge."

"Well, maybe you did. But you're letting it run away with you at the expense of our combat effectiveness. You guys went through the motions pretty good today, but the old zip was gone and you know it. Now all at once you think you're a bunch of saints because you're going to help a kid. And know why you're doing it?"

When nobody answered, Saunders went on. "Because in a way you're trying to make up for your original selfishness in exploiting the kid. And now that you see him as a prop for your better nature, a way to let yourself feel human again,

well, you're overdoing it when you let it affect the
unity of the squad. I'll tell you something, buddy-
ros, and I'll keep telling you this until the day they
roll me up in one of those mattress covers. First
things first in this outfit. That means we do our
combat job first. Anything else can come after.
So go ahead and give away all your goodies if it
makes you feel any better. But don't let it disrupt
the squad. Don't let it affect your relationships
with me or with each other. Have I made myself
clear?"

They all looked a little startled now, so Saunders hit the point one more time to be sure they
got it. "I'm still running the squad, this is still a
team, and that's the way it's going to be. You
think of the squad team first. You think of what
Chip Saunders wants and how he wants it. Then
if you got any thinking time left over, you can
worry about the human things."

Saunders looked at the little pile of contribu-
tions on the blanket. More than anything else he
wanted to add something of his own. But as pain-

ful as the urge was, and as starkly as he saw his own need to do it, he held back. The squad, he was sure, would see it as a cheap attempt to gain their favor, mark it as a sign of weakness, and forget the lesson he was trying to get through. So he simply said, "You can get that stuff to Keeno through Regimental Civil Affairs. Caje, let one man, no more, carry it up there."

Saunders looked at his watch, then said, "I have to go to a squad leaders' conference at company headquarters. Should be back in an hour. You guys all be here when I get back. I may have some important dope."

Picking up his helmet and slamming it onto his head, Saunders strode quickly out of the tent, not looking back, not pausing, but moving on to company headquarters with quick driving steps. As a result, he didn't hear Caje say in a low voice, "Everybody quiet about this now. Kirby, you know exactly where he is?"

"I know, Caje. I got it exact."

"Go get him. Sarge's going to get the mission.

And the boy goes with us. Sarge never knows the difference, right?"

A little chuckle rippled across the squad. Keeno would get to Germany yet. As a stowaway.

8

"DIRECT HIT!"

Saunders got the mission. Or most of it anyway. It gave him a funny feeling, not knowing exactly where they were going or the exact time, but that was how the airborne did it. Such vital details were held back until the very last minute, to keep any information from leaking to the enemy. Saunders was all the happier he'd gotten rid of Keeno. Be some stuff, wouldn't it, if they had a spy in their midst when the real hot dope came out? Nothing the Germans would like better than to know where the Nineteenth Airborne Division was going to drop.

The squad would be told in due time. Meanwhile, they got all the other details they needed because they were sealed in—moved to a staging area on the edge of the airfield and put on a strict alert so not a single man could leave the area. More security. But Saunders didn't mind. He used the time to get the squad ready. He ran them through a little catechism.

"What's the K Company mission, Brock?"

"Seize and secure Hill two-nineteen—wherever that is."

"Don't worry about that. You'll see maps and terrain models before long. Littlejohn, what's the platoon mission?"

"Assault platoon on the left flank. Outpost the left side of the hill when we seize the objective."

"Very good. Nelson, where's the company CP going to be ?"

"As far to the rear as possible."

That got a mild chuckle from the squad and Saunders said, "Very funny. So gimme twenty push-ups." It was a mild form of punishment Saunders had learned from the airborne, and as Nelson pumped up and down on the scant grass of the bivouac area, the squad counted the last few in unison: "Seventeen—eighteen—come *on,*

Nelse, you can do it—*NINE*teen—TUH-
WENTY!"

Saunders listened to the chatter with a critical
ear. He still wasn't satisfied they'd all bucked up
after the Keeno business, but you couldn't prove
anything. Nobody had said a word about the kid
since Saunders came back from the squad leaders'
conference that night after reading them off.
Maybe it was like he'd said—out of sight, out of
mind. And so it was a good thing. They could get
on with the war.

There were a lot of last-minute preparations
to get their minds off the little problems anyway.
They turned in all their letters, notebooks, diaries,
and personal papers for safekeeping so no intelligence items could fall into enemy hands. Most
of them drew at least one piece of new clothing,
mostly jackets or boots. They had their dog-tags
checked for at least the twentieth time. They
re-zeroed their weapons. Saunders personally
checked every rifle in the squad to make certain
that each man knew his sight settings and how to

hit what he was aiming at. "Gosh, Sarge," Kirby complained, "I got the zero of this piece down cold. I been lugging the thing ever since Normandy!"

"No bolos in this squad, Kirby. Zero it in and let me see a tight group on that target."

Kirby, grumbling that if he had a bolo knife he'd use it on Saunders, fired a clip as fast as he could work the trigger. When Saunders checked the target he slapped Kirby on the back. You could have covered the group of shots with a silver dollar. "Okay, Kirby. You're excused. We won't issue you a bolo after all. You're more dangerous with the rifle."

It was a hoary Army joke, this business about arming the poor shots with a bolo so they'd be more of a threat to the enemy than with a rifle, but it helped loosen everybody up. That was what Saunders wanted. As the time dragged on, they were beginning to tense up a little. The briefings, demonstrations, and lectures seemed interminable. They went through enemy identification, enemy weapons, and a variety of instruction until Littlejohn groaned. "This is worse than basic! Don't the Army know we been in this war already?"

"No such thing as too much dope, Littlejohn." Saunders spoke to the country boy but the words were intended for everybody. "This is for real, don't forget."

And at last they believed him. "Okay, gents." Finally Lieutenant Hanley assembled the platoon in front of a map and a terrain model covered with a big cloth. "Here's where we go. Take-off time tomorrow morning early, so's we can land about dawn. We'll do a little fatigue tonight helping load the paratroop cargo planes, then load up ourselves in time to get in right about daylight." He whisked the cloth off the map, a large scale projection with the Rhine River so big it looked like a tire tread twisted across the colored contours of a child's drawing. The terrain model was a three-dimensional mock-up of the same thing.

Picking up a pointer, the officer said, "Here's

the pure ungarbled word. We land across the Rhine River in the vicinity of Wesel"—he raised his eyebrows and surveyed the assembled platoon sardonically—"so the rumors were right after all, weren't they?" Then he went on saying, "And in case you think this is some cheap-jack enterprise let me advise you that the whole First Allied Airborne Army's involved in this thing. We're going to disrupt enemy communications, secure key road and canal crossings, and suck in a lot of the enemy's tactical reserves so the rest of the Allied troops can tee off on the Rhine-Siegfried attack to the south. So don't think there's not plenty of help going along. Because there is. This could be the last big push of the war."

He turned to the terrain model. "This is a little piece of Westphalia on the edge of Wesel. We go down here"—he pointed to a flat piece of ground just across the river—"and as soon as K Company's assembled, we light out for Hill two-nineteen which is a little farther to the northeast. It's the only real high ground on this side of town and you can't miss it. Now the captain says and the colonel says and everybody else says not to get bogged down in any fighting on the edge of the town here. Leave that for the follow-up. We have to bang right out there and grab that hill because it controls the route, this road over here, that the Krauts'll want to move reinforcements up on." He paused, looked around, and said, "See how simple it is?"

But it wasn't simple, because nothing ever is in war. Saunders knew that before they ever got off the ground in the marshaling area, but it didn't do any good. For one thing, some of the big C-47 aircraft, the twin-engine workhorses that carried the paratroopers and towed the gliders, had to abort. They were scrubbed from the mission because of engine trouble or maintenance failures, so the operation didn't get all the planes the plan called for. That meant there had to be more last minute changes in loading patterns than anyone had anticipated. The C-47's were going to take in paratroop loads, drop them, and then come back and tow some of the glider serials in. They couldn't land everybody simultaneously and, of course, they didn't tow the gliders behind the same planes that carried the paratroops. The paratroopers were dropped from lower altitudes anyway. The impact on Saunders and the squad was to put them in a tandem tow, two gliders behind one C-47. In what Lieutenant Hanley promised was the last and final change, Saunders and the squad found themselves ticketed for tandem tow in the first glider serial, which meant that now they would go in with the first paratroop waves where they'd been scheduled for the third serial before. The continual changing was somehow enormously irritating to Saunders.

"Holy cow, Lieutenant, I spent so much time running back and forth to get changes I haven't half supervised our own loading. I want to check every knot and lashing in that crate personally."

"That's okay," Lieutenant Hanley soothed him. "Caje is a good man. He's got you loaded up in fine shape. And you've got every bit of last-minute photo-intelligence, instructions, recognition signals, and fire-planning there is. And don't sweat that tandem tow drill. These pilots know what they're doing. Take the squad to chow. Last hot meal. They have steak for us. Then check the glider while there's light if you want, but sack in early. We're loading out at the marshaling area at o-three hundred hours."

The lieutenant was right, of course. When Saunders checked the glider he prowled over every inch of its cramped interior, Caje behind him, but each tie-down was solid, every knot was firm, and the jeep was lashed exactly right with respect to the center of gravity of the glider. Saunders patted the bulging tarp that covered the swelling load in the rear of the jeep, his fingers brushing the ropes that crisscrossed the canvas. "You check this personally, Caje? Everything looks good, but we don't want anything in the jeep to shift. It feels okay, but if anything's loose underneath it'd be bad."

"No strain, Sergeant. I loaded most of it by

myself. You'll be glad when you see how good a job we did."

Saunders nodded, patted the load one more time, then said, "Okay, then. Come on, let's flake out. We're making a pretty early start."

But there was more waiting. The take-off was delayed because of ground fog in the objective area across the Rhine in Germany. Somewhere up the line the command decision was made to risk the surprise that went with a dawn landing in favor of landing later in the morning in clear weather. Saunders sat in the lead seat of the glider, just behind the pilot's compartment, and tried to avoid looking at his watch. This was the hard part. The long sweat to get going.

There was a small porthole in the fuselage beside him and he could also look up the runway through the latticed Plexiglas nose of the glider. As always when an operation was getting under-way, Saunders had a vague sense of his helmet being too far down over his eyes so that an extra edge of shadow seemed cast over everything. It was an illusion, of course, because out on the runways, as far as he could see, the day was breaking with a clear crisp light that sharpened the long rows of C-47 aircraft echeloned alongside the strip to head into the runways, long nylon towcables snaked back to the gliders positioned behind them. The noise of the planes was incredible. It was a steady hammering at your ears that heightened the pulsing Saunders could feel inside his body. His belly was taut and he realized he was gripping his tommy gun between his knees with an uncommon strength. He blinked his eyes to shake off the shadow, turning to look at the squad ranged in the benchlike bucket seats on either side of the glider.

Caje was chewing gum with a slow working of his lean jaws, the black beret rolled up and thrust through a shoulder loop on his field jacket now that his steel helmet was a practical necessity. His bony hands were loose on his rifle, eyes staring straight ahead. Kirby, beside him, slumped forward against his seat belt, the airsickness pills already working on him. You could only hope he wouldn't still be groggy when they hit the landing zone. Like a lot of people, Kirby started to get airsick the minute he sat in the glider. It didn't even have to get off the ground.

Doc was watching Kirby, too, his red-crossed helmet tilted forward but his eyes were alert underneath. Saunders realized he was checking Kirby's breathing. Trust Doc to watch out for his boys. Littlejohn was cradling the BAR against his chest, feet pulled in close to clear the jeep that took up so much of the cargo space in the glider, while Corporal Nathaniel Davis, the hard-eyed jeep driver from company headquarters, fingered a hood-latch on the jeep for no apparent reason.

On the other bench, across the narrow aisle, Nelson was staring fixedly at a crate lashed to the floor and Saunders saw why. 5 ANTITANK MINES 5 the stencil on the crate read. Saunders smiled to himself. The lashing was okay, but he knew what Nelse was thinking: *What if . . . ?*

Brockmeyer, on the other hand, looked relaxed and was sitting there with his helmet in his lap, his stolid face impassive. "Get that hat on, Brock," Saunders said kindly. "You'll bash your head against a metal stanchion there."

Brockmeyer, not looking at Saunders, put his helmet on slowly and snapped the chin strap. Maybe it was heavy on your neck, Saunders thought, but in the practice flights he'd seen what the sudden bucking of a glider could do to throw a man against a metal fixture. He didn't want any casualties before they hit the ground.

Thinking about that reminded him of *flak*, the German antiaircraft fire they could expect to draw. Saunders was glad to see that every man was sitting on his trench shovel, a routine precaution they'd learned in training. There was always something funny about the idea of getting hit in the butt with a piece of steel but it wasn't funny when it happened to you. Saunders thought of the way the fabric of the glider dimpled the time Caje poked it with his finger. Nothing on the glider to keep out fragments. Sitting on your shovel was only common sense.

"Alert flare, Sergeant!" The glider pilot, a chunky Army Air Corps flight officer in a faded bush jacket passed the word to Saunders as a string of blue flares broke over the airport.

"All secure?" Saunders looked around at the squad, getting routine nods. They'd checked all they could already. But Saunders made himself take careful inventory. Seat belts snapped; all loads secure, even those ding-dong mines and the jeep. The men tensed forward now. Saunders felt his breath quicken. Ahead of them, on the far end of the runway, the first of the C-47's in their serial trundled forward.

Pop-pop-pop! Green flares snapped over the field. The noise outside flared into a high crescendo as C-47 throttles brought plane engines up to take-off tempo. Then, as Saunders watched, the planes started to take to the air. Slowly, gracefully, like a parade of giant predatory birds, the planes fled down the steel-planked strip and hurled themselves into the air, the gliders snatched after them on taut cables.

At last it was their turn.

With a sudden momentum that jerked them back in a head-snapping lash, their glider raced down the strip, sides vibrating in the prop-blast from the C-47 ahead, the pilot tense over his wheel-and-post control stick. The nylon tow cable was a thick umbilical connecting them to the plane, the glider so close to the ground on its stumpy landing gear that the steel planking of the field shot by under the wings with a dizzy unreeling that caught and held Saunders' eye in a hypnotic grasp. Then the strip suddenly fell away, and the rush of air hammering the sides of the glider changed tone as they were airborne.

"Made it!" Someone shouted the phrase as the squad let out its breath in a collective sigh. Twisting his head, Saunders looked out the port and saw the other glider in their tandem. It looked incredibly close. Saunders watched it buck and pitch with a flicker of sympathy until he realized that, of course, his own glider was acting the same way. The noise was different now that they were aloft, a thick dissonance made up of the scream of wires and struts, the flutter of fabric, and the drumming of the prop-blast from the airplane ahead. The wings were vibrating violently now, the pilot fighting the control post to break up the tail-flutter, a quirk of glider aerodynamics that could shake the thing to pieces if you didn't catch it.

"Look, Ma, no engine!" That was Littlejohn, trying to relax everybody, but just as he got the words out, the glider gave a tremendous lurch. Saunders' belly seemed to detach itself from his body as his seat fell away from him. Then he hit his seat and his shovel with a jarring wallop as the glider came back up while he was going down and they rose straight up. Gritting his teeth, Saunders tried to keep his seat. *Wouldn't you know it?* he thought. The turbulence was the worst it had ever been.

But you had to live with it, and it couldn't last

forever. It only seemed that way. Ahead of them, seen through the nose, the serial stretched as far as the eye could see, a long column of aircraft winging into a sky that at this altitude seemed uncommonly blue. Below them, the ground looked smooth and hazy, glazed with a faint mist. Somehow it was hard to imagine there was any danger down there. A huge river, a twisting blade carving through the softness, came into view and then dropped slowly behind them. That would be the Seine, Saunders knew. He pictured a big map in his mind. Next would be the Maas River and then—he swallowed, throat feeling harsh and dry—the Rhine.

For what seemed like an eternity, the squad swung and dipped above the land, small comfort in the impressive display of power represented by the huge air serial, the fighter planes on high cover that occasionally flashed into view far above them, or even in the knowledge that they were as ready as they ever could be to take part in a big battle stretching a hundred or more miles along the ground. As always, it was the unknowns that worried Saunders. What did the Krauts have down there? Was the intelligence right? Did the squad have a good chance of making it through?

You might be part of the big picture way up here in the sky, churning and lurching through the air, but when you got down there on the ground, you got in awful tight focus. It didn't make any difference what everyone else was doing. The whole war suddenly seemed to zero in on you personally. No matter how much experience you had, it never got any better each time you got into the action.

Pop! Crack! Bup-bup-bup! New sounds cut through the sustained hammering of the slipstream at the fragile ribs of the glider. Caje poked Saunders on the shoulder, gesturing. Looking out along the serial, Saunders saw little black puffs of smoke blooming like some deadly flower at varying altitudes, floating toward them with agonizing slowness to disappear for an instant before they were replaced by others.

Flak!

Saunders tried to remember that the briefings had told them to expect antiaircraft fire, that there was an air cover plan to reduce this, and the odds of your getting hit were long. But it didn't do any good. It was a frightening thing, sitting there helpless. You tried to duck and dodge, but there was no place to go. Those black blossoms kept coming up, planted by the Kraut ack-ack guns far below. Incredibly, from time to time, Saunders could see little flickers of fire in the ground carpet down there. For a moment he thought they were fires started by their own cover aircraft. Then he realized he was seeing the muzzle bursts of the guns themselves, the wicked plants that created the blossoms now thickening around them.

"*Aoowww!*" A weird screech from somebody made Saunders shiver. For a sick moment he thought someone was hit, then he saw what prompted the scream.

Ahead of them, with a heart-stopping awkwardness, a C-47 turned slowly out of the serial in a long arc, thick smoke pluming out of its belly, the twin tow cables trailing loosely, now like ugly intestines streaming from the gutted craft. Its two gliders peeled off in a lesser arc, and even from this distance, Saunders could see the lumbering heaviness of their spiraling descent.

As the C-47 went down in its long slant, one—two—three—four men bailed out. Shortly they were swinging on parachutes, sliding below the glider like floating white mushrooms among the flak bursts. So the plane crew got out all right.

But Saunders held his breath for the gliders. They were so cussed slow—great logy things. As much as he hated to watch, Saunders couldn't tear his eyes away. A surging anger seized him; he cursed his own helplessness. With a gentle almost offhand drifting, the flak bursts started to cluster around the one glider Saunders could still see. *Phoooom!* There was a direct hit.

The glider must have had gasoline as part of its load because it burst into an uneven wad of flame that curled wings and tail section into a crumpling crisp. The helpless men inside fell away like caterpillars dropping out of a burning nest. Saunders couldn't count them, the saliva roiling in his throat somehow affected his eyes. As his own glider passed overhead, he was conscious only of the fact that the men seemed to be falling very slowly and there seemed to be a great many of them. None of them had parachutes.

Shaking his head to clear it, Saunders turned back to the squad. They'd all seen it, apparently, because Nelse was giving a series of little screeches. Davis, the jeep driver, slapped him quickly across the face to snap him out of it while Brockmeyer was being noisily sick in his helmet. Caje was saying a brief prayer and Kirby, eyes glazed, stared hollowly at Saunders. Doc was twisting at a porthole, obviously trying to count the men that were clawing their way down. Littlejohn seemed to be trying to get the BAR up to where he could fire down on the Krauts below.

Taking this all in, Saunders did the only thing

he could think of. "Listen, you guys," he bellowed above the noise in the glider. "Listen! I want five Krauts for every one of those poor birds. You hear me? Five Krauts for every one! *Five!*"

It wasn't much. But somehow it helped.

9

"READY AS WE'LL EVER BE. . . ."

When Saunders cleared his head and looked through the Plexiglas again, he saw that his perspective was changing a little because they were losing altitude. He saw the Rhine looming ahead of them in a sluggish kaleidoscope, the rough geometry of the ground spreading now into the distant haze in a shifting pattern of greens, browns, faint yellows, and the occasional black emphasis of a road. An irregular heavy blur, he decided, was either Wesel or Dortmund, he wasn't sure which.

"Going down!"

The glider pilot lifted his hand in a signal, then reached forward and jerked the cable release lever. The tow cable fell away and the glider turned in a long bank, the sounds softening instantly to a gentle gushing as the airspeed fell off. Saunders had a confused picture of the land below pinwheeling around the nose of the glider as they went down, a multicolored view of bursting flak, land tones, a flash of the river, and then a long close-up of pasture and fencing followed by a jarring thump and rattling roll as the glider went screeching down in an incredibly bumpy landing.

In a confusion of yelling men, gliders sailing overhead, swirling smoke, and the heavy movements of nightmare, they got the glider nose open and everybody out.

Saunders took a quick look around, trying to recognize the orientation points they'd been briefed on. As near as he could tell, they'd hit their proper landing zone okay. The orange smoke signals planted by the pathfinders who jumped in advance of the paratroopers were drifting out of a small patch of woods to his distant right. While he couldn't see the Rhine, they were in a long rectangular pasture crisscrossed with shallow fencing that had claimed two gliders already, nosed over with tails high. To his immediate right Saunders saw the cluster of buildings that marked the town they were supposed to keep out of. Wesel, probably.

"On the jeep, everybody! Davis, head for that road over there." He signaled the driver to a dirt road along the edge of the pasture, taking a chance there were no mines. This was the hard part, because Checkerboard Blue and K Company were all scattered. Until he got his bearings, Saunders knew the smart thing to do was to get close to cover, pull the squad together and prepare to bang on forward toward Hill 219 as soon as they had some tactical integrity.

As they made the road Saunders saw that they had plenty of company. The terrain around him was gently rolling, and as far as he could see, the ground was spotted with gliders in various crazy postures. Parachutes were all over the place, and fragmentary columns were either moving out as part of an overall plan or pulling together to preserve firepower and strength the way you had to do when things were uncertain.

A thin cluster of buildings pressed against the road where the jeep bucked the ditch, long low structures with whitewashed stone walls and rough thatching on the roofs, sitting in a tangle of fencing, farm implements, and cobbled ramps. Saunders recognized this as a *bauerhof*, a farm village, and the cover of the nearest shed was a good place to get pulled together. Apparently the airborne drop was unopposed but Saunders didn't kid himself; it could be just a matter of moments before they got socked with artillery if nothing else.

Saunders held a swift consultation with Caje over the map he pulled from inside his shirt. "I make the objective that blob on the skyline, Caje. That looks like Hill two-nineteen to me. You agree?"

Caje consulted his compass, then nodded. "That must be it. It's the right azimuth."

They were kept from further discussion by a

jeep that came hustling up behind them, Major O'Connors, the battalion operations officer, bouncing in the seat. The jeep slowed to a halt, the major saying, "What outfit's this?" Then his eyes lit up and he said, "It's Saunders, isn't it? K Company? Good. Battalion's assembling right around this farm. I'll run the rest of K in on you. Battalion headquarters is right around the bend, in the farmhouse proper. Post local security for now, Saunders. Get your jeep unloaded there, and we'll be in business right away. If you see any more Checkerboard people, shoot them in here. We got down in pretty good style, but we're a little scattered, is all."

The major took off in a burst of speed and Saunders turned to Caje. "That makes it a little easier. We must have landed ahead of the company somehow. Okay, let's get the jeep unloaded, and—" Saunders paused because Caje looked strange. "What's the matter, Caje? You got battle fatigue already? You heard what the major said."

"That's what is worrying me." Caje moved

slowly to the jeep and then said in a loud voice, "Okay, squad! Everybody on the jeep. Turn to!"

Saunders, studying his map and checking the terrain, didn't pay any attention to the squad beyond saying, "Doc, be sure everybody's okay." But it was such an automatic thing with Doc to do that Saunders didn't even bother to look at him. Instead he concentrated on his map, deciding that the *bauerhof,* the farm village, was really an extension of the city proper, and therefore that had to be the objective out there on the skyline. Lot of open country from here to there. That was the only hard part. And if they got counterattacked. . . .

"Sergeant Saunders." Caje was being strangely formal and then, when Saunders raised his eyes from the map, he saw why. For an instant he couldn't believe what he saw. Then the blind fury seized him. "Caje," he said, a vicious bite to the word, "I'll have every man in this squad in front of a court-martial! How in the blue flaming blazes did *he* get here?"

Crawling out from under the jeep tarp, blinking and obviously stiff in every joint, his GI field jacket incredibly rumpled, pale face like chalk, a feeble smile responding to the cheerful greetings of the squad, came Keeno. "Hullo, chaps," he was saying. "Awfully good of you to help me like this. It wasn't half bad in there, truly it wasn't."

"Keeno!" Saunders bellowed at him so loud the boy winced visibly. "You're a stowaway! Davis—Caje—everyone of you—you knew about this all the time! Well sound off, somebody! What by all that's holy do you—"

Wump! Wump! Wump! Without warning the landing area was blanketed with fire. Great bursts of black smoke gushed out of the ground, fragments snarled and whined. *Clang! Clang! Clang!* the odd gonging sound of a close-in sheaf deafened Saunders momentarily. It was Kraut mortar fire, big stuff, probably 120 millimeter or more.

"Take cover! In that shed! Get that jeep out of here!" This was serious, you could tell by the pattern slamming all around them. It wasn't some-

thing you could duck by hitting the dirt. Buildings were better. Saunders waited a long moment while the squad raced into the barnyard in longlegged strides. Then as he raced after them *Zzzhyew! Zzzhyew! Zzzhyew!* the peculiar lowkeyed whine of *nebelwerfers* bit through the throaty sound of the mortars.

"Screaming meemies!" Kirby, any grogginess driven away now, lay on his belly against the thick wall of the wagon shed as Saunders plunked down beside him. "We ain't seen them in a while!" *Zzzhyew! Zzzhyew! Zzzyhew!* The *nebelwerfers* were a sort of rocket that came in from a flat angle and burst in long shallow cones so that with the mortar fire they made an effective rolling curtain nothing could live under. The din in the *bauerhof* was terrific now. The acrid smoke made your eyes water. There was nothing to do but lie there and take it and hope your number wasn't on any of the stuff roaring in. All thought of Keeno and the squad's part in letting him stow away were driven from Saunders' mind now.

He was trying to figure out what to do; he was trying to figure out if he actually could do anything. Nothing was worse than being pinned down by artillery or mortar fire. You couldn't fight back, you didn't dare get up and move, all you could do was lie there and take it. Your body bucked and slammed against the ground, the continual concussion felt like large fingers squeezing your head. The constant *Wump! Wump! Zzzhyew! Zzzhyew! Zzzhyew!* was so terrorizing as to drain every thought out of you except the hope that you could stay alive.

But you had to fight that if you were really going to stay alive. Because this was observed fire. The Krauts were reacting now to the airborne drop. They fired mortars and screaming meemies when they could see the strike and adjust it. Somewhere out there around them Krauts were watching. They'd shift the fire to where it could best break up the assembly of the airborne outfits. And gradually, as his head was slammed against the soft footing of the shed, as the tiled roofing above him was punctured and torn, as the firing reached an almost unbearable pitch, Saunders was aware of movement around him and looked up to see Major O'Connors, followed by Lieutenant Hanley, come running through the doorway, crouching low.

Then, as if cued by their arrival, the hammering fire moved on behind them through the *bauerhof,* stalking more prey elsewhere in the drop area, but now making it possible to talk in reasonable tones. Major O'Connors put a hand on Lieutenant Hanley's shoulder. "I can't contact K Company Commander," the major said. "I don't know whether they got lost in the glider drop or what. But there's a change in orders because we've gotten word there's a counterattack coming up." He shook his head wearily. "We'd have done better to get in here at daylight and take our chances on the fog. The Krauts are moving down on us in strength. So we're going to defend right here. I want this platoon to maintain this position and keep contact with me for sure. This is a vital approach, across the pasture here. Think you can do that, Hanley? Saunders?"

"Yes, sir." Saunders spoke first.

"Fine business. Now let me borrow that jeep. I just lost mine." Then, as the jeep rolled over in response to Saunders' signal the major said in a strange voice, "Isn't that the refugee we had some trouble with back in France? I thought he was at Civil Affairs." The major looked at Keeno, then at Hanley. "I'm sure it is. You had him in tow, Hanley. What's he doing here?"

Lieutenant Hanley looked both blank and embarrassed. Saunders felt the unspoken pressure of the squad on him. It was a weird time and place to start any arguments over Keeno, wasn't it? So Saunders took a deep breath, then said, "Major, it's a long story and I don't think there's time to go into it now. Let's just say I'm responsible for his being here and I'll be responsible for getting him out. That do it for now, sir?"

"Well, yes, of course, Sergeant." The major grinned. "When things get tough, put a rifle in his hand. We may need him. I'll be in touch. Give me a call over the radio net when your defense is in. You're all we've got of K Company, so far as I know."

As the major rolled out of the yard in the jeep, Lieutenant Hanley said to Saunders, "We're awful thin. I keep hoping the rest of the company will show up. They must have gotten spread out too much."

Saunders, thinking of the gliders he'd seen shot down on the way in, said, "You think they made it down?"

"Gee, I think so." He paused, then said, "But we got our own problems now. Here's what we'll do." He moved with Saunders to the edge of the shed, saying, "I've made a pretty good check of this *bauerhof,* or whatever they call it. If you rig your mortar to cover this open field from the little woods on the right to the line of trees along the road there on the left, that'll make a good sector for you. The major thinks any counter-attack will come straight down the axis of the road beyond Hill two-nineteen, the one we were supposed to cut. If it does, it'll hit the other battalion, not us. But if they do any maneuvering at all, you're apt to get a force right in through here."

"What do we do then?"

"Break it up if you can. If you can't, withdraw back on Major O'Connors and we'll shrink the perimeter. Get into radio contact soon's you can so we can keep in touch."

"What's with all these buildings? They clear?"

"So far as I know. See, they're laid out in a sort of piece-of-pie shape. This batch right along the road is the arc of the crust, then they narrow back to a point where the major is."

"I can take up the best position I want, though, is that right?"

"Oh, yes. But cover out here good. I'll check with you later."

Saunders thought a moment. The mission wasn't to his liking at all because the squad was trying to take in too much ground with what they had. But it wasn't the first time this had happened and it wouldn't be the last so the thing to do was to get with it. But there was one other item. "You couldn't scare me up a bazooka team, could you? If the Krauts do come in here they're bound to have some tanks or anyway some kind of armored vehicle. We don't have much anti-tank stuff except five mines over there in some of the company stuff. I don't hardly dare put them out in case some of our own people have to pull back through them."

The lieutenant rubbed a hand along his chin, looking thoughtful. "I can pry a bazooka team out of the major. L Company can send it over." He looked at a map he unfolded from his pocket, then said, "See here on the map? That's a little stream line at a culvert in the road down there, maybe a couple hundred yards. Where the ground dips. Check it out and if it's a good place to put the mines, go ahead. Just let me know." He folded his map and put it away, then said, "Way I get it, the whole outfit got scattered toward the south and west, sort of tight against the river. The Krauts are mostly north and east. So that's the threat out there. I still think we have an edge on them if we can get everybody pulled together. That's the hard part. You shouldn't have to hold here too long."

"How long, do you think?"

"Hard to say. Not more'n a day. I hope."

"You hope."

"Yeah." Lieutenant Hanley looked at Saunders for a long moment, then said, "We both hope."

"Okay. I'll get with it."

"I'll have a bazooka team up here as soon as I can."

Saunders had a lot to get done and he started several things going at once, not only because time was all-important, but because you couldn't be sure of the complete picture. If they got pasted once with mortars and screaming meemies they could get pasted again. They were under observation from somewhere, unless their own artillery (if it had gotten in) or the air cover could blind the observation. There were a million worries and time to deal with only a few. So Saunders gave some crisp orders, getting everybody moving.

"Nelson, you take your little buddy Keeno and check these buildings. They're supposed to be clear but don't bet on it. I don't want any Krauts behind me. Let him cover you if you have to. He wants to play airborne, let him work at it. Kirby, you get on that walkie-talkie and you get us contact with battalion or somebody that'll talk English to us. Littlejohn, you and Brockmeyer stake out the BAR and the mortar. I want to cover from that woods on the right to that tree line along the road there on the left. Caje, you come with me. I want to do a little fast reconnaissance by that culvert. Doc, you help Littlejohn and Brock. I'll be back here in fifteen minutes. Maybe less."

Saunders moved briskly off the line of buildings along the edge of the road, keeping a sharp eye for mines. Now that they were actually doing something, he thought he was getting a feel for the bigger picture. They had probably gotten some tactical surprise with the airborne drop. But getting scattered, they didn't have enough momentum yet as a major force to bang out to the specified objectives. So they'd pull themselves together, then do it. Maybe tonight, maybe tomorrow. Meanwhile the Krauts were reacting. In a way, it was a race with time. To see if the Krauts could roll them up or if they could hold the Krauts off. Saunders shook his head as he moved along the spongy sod on the edge of the road at the ditch. Only thing was, you could get killed just as dead that way as you could in a big, big deal. It wasn't the size of the operation that mattered; it was how it affected you personally.

"Thank you, Sergeant, for what you did." Behind him, Caje was talking in a low voice. "It was a good thing."

"What are you talking about, you crummy bayou jumper?"

"Not getting sore about the boy. You stood up well for him with the major."

Saunders didn't bother to turn his head. "I got more on my mind right now than finding out why you guys thought you had to pull a fast one on me. Think I sent him with Kirby for fun? I want someone to keep an eye on him every clinking minute. And I'll tell you something else. One false move out of him and I'll cut him in two." Saunders gestured with his tommy gun. "And I wouldn't bat an eye. You got it?"

"I got it." Caje's voice sounded heavy with disbelief but Saunders told himself he meant every word he said. Then he focused on something ahead that had to do with the task at hand.

"Look, Caje. See how that little swale slopes down and then back up in a little half-moon, on the far side of the culvert there? It looks like an old dam or something. Or else it's some kind of overflow area. May be a little mushy but that's a perfect breastworks on the left. And I'll tell you something else."

"What's that?"

"I like it better than that farm village. That

bauerhof's on the map, the Krauts are already zeroed in on it. They may have even surveyed their artillery in. But this culvert area's something they'd have to sense for. It'd be a hair safer from a cover point of view. We'd get a better enfilade on that approach we have to watch. I'm going to put the squad in here. You agree?"

Caje looked around for a long moment, then said, "I think you got it, Sergeant."

"Okay, go get the squad. Bring them up low on the far side of the road, let them belly in here the last few yards. They can make it unobserved. I'll stay here and check it out, then place each man as he comes up."

Saunders was pleased with the idea and so some of his confidence returned. While Caje was getting the squad up, Saunders saw that the ground shaped itself into a small natural fort with the stream bed in the middle. From the tiny stream a curved rib of ground swept back perhaps a hundred yards long and a good fifty yards from the road itself. At the road, the stream pooled a little now but wasn't high enough to go through the culvert, which was a very long and rather narrow pipe. Instead of ending immediately on the other side of the road like most culverts, this pipe ran another twenty or thirty yards straight under, then on past the road. Though it was covered with marshy weeds and so almost concealed, Saunders saw that it ended over there in a little spillway. The farmers probably used the water for irrigation of some sort when the stream was higher. Then it occurred to him that it could be a hiding place for Krauts, so he took the trouble to check it.

The position was potentially so good he didn't want to take any chances of its use being denied him so he scrambled down and took a careful look into the pipe. It was clear though; he thought he glimpsed daylight at the other end. It looked too small for a man to get into anyway, so dismissing it as a risk, he went back to the problem of laying out the squad.

By the time the last man had come crawling up over the road and flopped into the crescent-

shaped position Saunders was reasonably happy
with his dispositions. He put Brockmeyer with the
mortar in back, with Keeno told off to help him.
"Make him work, Brock," Saunders warned.
Littlejohn posted the BAR on the left, while Nelson had a good rifle position on the breastworks.
Caje brought up the bazooka team himself, twin
brothers oddly enough, replacements in L Company assigned to the same outfit by the Army
policy that kept twin brothers together where-
ever possible. They were alike as two of their own
bazooka rounds. "We're the Dunns," one of them
said. "I'm Alan and he's Neal. You want anything
bazooka'd, Sergeant, we can sure do it."

They were dark, competent-looking soldiers
and they wasted no time sighting the bazooka to
cover the road while Caje flopped down beside
Saunders on the breastworks. "You want to do
any digging?"

"Yeah. What we can. Kirby get in the net?"

"We have the problems with him. The walkie-
talkie fades in and out here."

"It does?" Saunders turned to Kirby, crouched against the road embankment, the walkie-talkie to his face. "Any luck there, Kirby?"

Kirby shook his head. "Can't get anybody now. I'll move around a little. I had battalion back there at the farm five by five."

Saunders mumbled to himself. The radio was sensitive to location, and maybe the position was too low for the signals to come in properly to the little extendable antenna. "Try a little higher up on the road. We *got* to get in that net."

Kirby finally got in by going clear across the road toward the far end of the culvert, from where he signaled an okay with circled thumb and fingers. Saunders sighed a small sigh, then looked around the position. "Where's Doc, Caje? I almost forgot about him."

"I sent him to Lieutenant Hanley for some fire plans. He should be here soon."

Doc showed up a few moments later and handed Saunders a map overlay along with a written message from Lieutenant Hanley. The overlay had some fire concentrations marked on it, and the message confirmed that the force was getting itself collected with a view to moving out on its assigned objectives late in the day. Meanwhile, the platoon was still all that was available of K Company because the balance of the company was moving up from well to the south where it had gotten scattered. *Use the battalion command net*, the message concluded, *and hold out as long as you can.*

Well, Saunders thought, it was nice to know that K Company was still intact, even if it was badly scattered. He stuck the overlay on his map to mark in the fire plan but first he took another look around the position. We're as ready as we'll ever be, he told himself. Let's just hope the Krauts don't push us too hard.

10

"COUNTERATTACK!"

Were the Krauts out there or weren't they?

It was the waiting and wondering that was tough. Saunders lay on the moist grass of the breastworks, head just high enough so he could peep through the rippling barley or whatever it was. The ground had a fresh smell, perhaps because of the water nearby. Somehow it reminded him of when he was a boy and he used to lie in the grass for hours looking at the sky and wondering what it was that made clouds. Just as the limitless space of the sky used to challenge him then, now the shapeless unknowns of the war pressed in on him, and he tried to find some comfort to offset the deep-seated fear gripping him low in the belly.

He looked for some refuge in the fact that this

was Germany. At last they were on German soil. But the land looked very much like other ground they had covered. It could have been France, maybe a part of pastoral England where they trained before the invasion, even a piece of the United States. Hill 219 was perhaps a mile to his far right, a soft swelling on the gentle land that rolled and dipped to an uneven skyline. There was little to give the land any distinctive cast. Except for the gliders and parachutes strewn in the vicinity of the *bauerhof,* there was nothing but the fencing, slight variation in shades of green, the scattered trees, and a road to give the land any character.

So it was the threat of the Krauts, somewhere off in the distance, that created the fear. The familiarity of the sensation didn't help any. It was not a thing you welcomed. Saunders knew from long experience how the threat in its various manifestations colored his judgment, trying to overwhelm him by sheer weight of terror. He knew that his real strength against this lay in the squad.

They depended on each other. This had been proven in countless ways already in the war and they all knew it. None of them would do anything to let the rest of them down. That was what kept them going, what gave the squad its positive meaning. That was what helped them overcome the great unknowns that were pressing in on them.

Saunders, as squad leader, had to know more about this than anyone because it was his orders and his decisions that moved them from minute to minute and hour to hour through the dangers of the war, giving guidance and, to this squad, spirit. The business with Keeno had fractured this spirit from the beginning, because the squad saw the boy in one light and Saunders saw him in yet another. All of them, Saunders was sure, knew the risks this split gave to their squad unity. Thinking about it, he supposed that the reason the squad let Keeno stow away on the glider was out of some mistaken idea that this was the way to retrieve the squad status as it existed in its own eyes before

Saunders accused them of being no better than the Germans.

Lying there, his body pressing the earth, sweating out the situation, Saunders knew that somehow something had to give. You never owned very much in a war, not even your own body. That was at the mercy of your mission and the events that swirled and roiled around you. So whenever you survived this storm and thunder, you didn't survive by yourself. You survived because your buddies helped you. And what was so remarkable was, they all saw it that way. They all *belonged* to the squad and so they *belonged* to each other. The value of that belonging had been proof-tested hundreds of times over this far in the war already. It was this loyalty serving mutual need that was so important, being the only thing you really did own. Therefore, Saunders saw with a sudden clarity, when you fooled around with it, you were taking chances with the most precious thing you had in this war.

So even if the other men in the squad all knew

about Keeno in the glider, as certainly they must have for the kid to work the flight the way he did, they were trying to give some of this strength and loyalty to someone else who needed it badly, thereby boosting their own strength. It was as simple as that.

It didn't matter that they did it awkwardly, with some deception and with a lack of forethought as to how it might all work out. The important thing was, they were trying to share their greatest strength. Doing it the way they did, they left it open for Saunders to go along with them. They had given him other chances, and he had rejected them all. When Kirby brought the boy in, back in France; when the lieutenant said the kid should stay; when they gave Keeno their pitiful little gifts. Each time Saunders had the chance to go along and he turned his back on them. So now that Keeno was in Germany, now that he'd been smuggled in, so to speak, was it the right thing to do, thinking how important the squad spirit was, to turn your back on them again? That was the question you had to answer. You couldn't duck.

But you couldn't answer it here either. Not while you were leaning forward against the unknown, waiting for something to happen any minute. The Krauts knew they were there, had put heavy fire on the *bauerhof* already. It was just a question of time before the Krauts came banging in. They hadn't run the airborne off with mortar fire and the screaming meemies. They'd have to do it with troops. But when?

The answer was not long in coming.

"Sarge! At three o'clock! On the hill!" Caje sounded the warning.

Saunders focused on the hill, shading his eyes with his hand. There was indistinct movement there, a vague milling of a handful of figures. It could be some kind of fire support going in, but it was hard to make out anything definite.

"Hey, Sarge!" Kirby materialized beside Saunders, walkie-talkie in hand. "We just got a radio message. Heavy attack building up in front of the other battalion. Look out for a diversionary effort here, the batallion says!"

"Yeah, I got it. Tell 'em we can see movement, unidentified, on Hill two-nineteen. We'll continue to observe."

Then, as Kirby chattered into the mouthpiece, Saunders watched him anxiously, then said, "Can't you raise 'em from here?"

Kirby smacked the heel of his hand against the little set, and gave the call sign again. "Checkerboard Blue, this is King Two One. Checkerboard Blue, this is King Two One. Do you read me? Do you read me? Over!" He waited a moment, listening, face tense, then said, "I can't raise 'em here, Sarge. I'll go back where I was. I can get 'em there."

"Okay, Kirby. Spit on the battery terminals or something. We want to get through!"

Wump! Wump! Wump! Crrrr-ack! Ack! Ack! As though to underline the urgency of Saunders' order, a thick curtain of fire rippled over the field. Saunders, flattening himself in the shallow hole he'd scooped out of the angle of the breastworks,

knew there was no need to signal the squad to cover. The incoming mail did that. The heck of it was, this was mostly artillery fire, with mortar fire interspersed. Kraut artillery made a harsher blast than the throatier explosion of the mortars. Saunders forced himself to keep his head up to try and verify the pattern of the fire, and likewise, to see if the Krauts were running any infantry in behind it. The main target seemed to be the *bauer-hof* to his far left, but this was at least a battery salvo, and stuff was hitting murderously close to the squad from the spread.

"Okay, you guys! Get Set! Counterattack!" Saunders shouted the command as a reflex to the sudden heart-stopping development in front of him. Out in the gentle sweep of the pasture, still well beyond effective rifle range, Kraut infantry was deploying out of shallow approaches probably fed from back of Hill 219. It was at least a platoon. Twenty, maybe twenty-five men.

At a distance they looked small, tiny figures in *feld-grau* long coats flapping over baggy trousers, coal-bucket helmets a blurred silhouette. They looked to be moving in an approach formation, roughly in a line of squad columns. They were apparently oriented on the *bauerhof*.

In the instant he had to size up the situation, Saunders saw that they were following about as close to the slamming artillery as you could expect. Their general direction showed they didn't know Saunders and the squad were there, or else they chose to ignore them, which, of course, wasn't likely. Their size, while outnumbering the squad, made it apparent they were probably a reconnaissance in force. That'd be smart on the part of the Krauts. If the airborne drop caught them by surprise at all, if they were making a main effort against the other battalion, then they could be thinking that their original fire pattern on the *bauerhof* followed up by this pasting and a few foot troops would take care of this end of the action.

So there was one good way to deal with this. Artillery fire.

Saunders took a quick look at his map overlay, then turned his head. He yelled back to Brockmeyer, "Tell Kirby to ask for number thirty-four. Thuh-ree-four! Kraut infantry! Platoon strength!"

In a matter of moments, Doc bellied his way to Saunders. "Kirby says he can't get 'em on the radio anymore!" He ducked his head as a bracket of fire crashed on the road behind them. Over in the *bauerhof* the shells slammed through tile roofs and stucco walls, generating a big cloud of dust and a pall of gray smoke. "He's still trying!"

Saunders banged a fist on the ground in frustration. He hated to expose his position this early. If the Krauts got into the *bauerhof* there'd be trouble for everybody. The squad would get cut off. And obviously, if he opened fire from here, the squad would be the target for artillery and infantry that outnumbered them in firepower and men. But there was no real choice. Saunders quickly crawled to Brockmeyer at the mortar. "Let's go to work, Brock! Range, eight hundred yards. Five rounds. Fire when ready."

Keeno stared anxiously at Saunders, but the Sergeant ignored him as Brockmeyer twiddled with his cross-leveling, peered at his aiming stake, then looked into the sight. "Too far, Sarge. That'll be way over!"

"Not much, you ninny! They can't tell where mortar fire comes from! They'll think it's from the farm there. I want to drive them this way for cover!"

Quickly, Brockmeyer and Doc fed the tear-shaped rounds Keeno handed them into the tube, setting the increments carefully, slapping the ammunition down the spout. *Koff! Koff! Koff-koff-koff!*

Saunders, back at the breastworks, scanned the field anxiously. It seemed to take hours for the mortar shells to land. Meanwhile, the enemy artillery looked to be searching on beyond the *bauerhof* and to its far side. Saunders gulped. That meant it could come searching their way any minute.

Then their own mortars burst like cotton bolls

on the ground out in front. Not a bad group, considering they hadn't registered the mortar before, but Saunders couldn't tell how many Krauts the bursts took down. The Krauts milled around a little, but they didn't immediately take any cover, which was a good index to their combat skill. The mortars didn't bother them enough. There had to be more. Saunders couldn't tell if they were going to change direction or not.

"Drop range fifty," he hollered at Brock. "Give 'em five rounds, then drop fifty again and five more. Fast as you can!"

Then Saunders dashed over to where the Dunn brothers crouched at their bazooka. "How much maximum effective range can you get out of that sewer pipe?"

One of them, Alan or Neal, Saunders didn't know which, spoke up confidently. "Three hundred yards, if we aim it high."

"You see those Krauts out there?"

"You bet."

"When they get to that line of fencing out

there—see, the white posts and the wire?—that's about two-hundred-fifty yards—I'm going to give them everything we got. You flip as many of those rockets in there as you can. What you got in there now?"

"Armor-piercing."

"You got any HE? Any white phosphorus?"

"Four HE, two white phosphorous."

"Good. Shoot the HE first on my order. Then lay the white phosphorus in there."

When Saunders got back to where he could observe, Brockmeyer's mortar fire was having some effect. The Kraut formation wavered, and changed direction. A few men went down. Then, as they moved toward the fence line, Saunders gave his firing orders crisply, the excitement of the action boiling up in him now. "Remember what I said about the glider! I want five Krauts apiece."

And for a moment it looked like it would work. Littlejohn's BAR chattered. Rifles bucked. The bazooka rounds splattered the Krauts with a hammering high explosive. The phosphorous rounds burst with incredible whiteness to put smoke down while searing any Kraut in its way.

The Krauts faltered near the fence line, but they recovered quickly. The smoke hung low, but not low enough to obscure them. They built their firing line up rapidly. Now the *duh-duh-duh ka-pow! ka-pow!* of Kraut gunfire slammed into the squad position, kicking up blobs of dirt, cracking overhead with the surprising ballistic concussion small-arms fire has. Saunders sickened at the frightening sound of the high cyclic rate of the Kraut weapons. The nausea was compounded when shortly the artillery fire shifted and they got blasted with high explosive. It came in suddenly, with no audible whistle. *Crrr-ack! ack! Ooom-poom-poom!* In a matter of minutes, the squad was pinned down. Tight.

It was a gut-watering sensation. Small arms snapped and whined overhead, forcing your head down with the shock of a physical blow, so close did the vicious cracking come. Huge fragments of artillery snarled and whirred through the air. The noise was horrendous, a cacophony of hell that sent you grinding against the dirt, making you claw and scrabble with your hands.

Saunders, forcing himself to raise his head so he could see, knew there were only two choices. Stay there and get overrun, or get some fire support down on the Krauts at the fence line.

Quickly he checked the squad. Caje was huddled forward on his rifle, snapping shots when he could. A big rip in his steel helmet showed how close the gunfire was coming. Littlejohn gripped the BAR, reaching around from a face-down position, firing short bursts and traversing. Nelson lay twitching. Hit? Then Saunders saw he was flicking off shots one-handed, so he was still active anyway. The Dunn twins were methodically feeding rounds into the bazooka from prone positions, but their ammunition wouldn't last long. Back at the mortar Brock crouched deep on the edge of the stream against the banking of the road, Keeno and Doc flattened in the mud. Brock held up five fingers to Saunders. Five rounds left.

Only one solution. Kirby had to get through on the radio. Saunders wormed his way swiftly to an embankment at the road and raised up enough to yell at Kirby, then saw it wouldn't do any good. Kirby lay slack at the far end of the culvert, one hand gently flapping toward Saunders.

"Doc!" Saunders whirled. "Kirby's hit! Can you get to him? We got to get that radio!"

"I'll try!" But no sooner had the little medic started up the embankment than another salvo of artillery crashed into the road. He darted back to the safety of the cover. "I'll never make it under that!"

Saunders, fighting the desperation gripping him, started to go himself but then another blast blew him literally backward.

Groggily Saunders shook his head. He was okay, he could tell that. Shaken a bit, no damage. *Whang! Whang! Whang!* The fire was murderous. How long could they last?

"Sergeant! Sergeant! What fire numbers do you

want?" Someone was yelling in Saunders' face, a mud-spattered little pixie.

"Keeno! What can you do?"

Suddenly Keeno spoke in the pure patois of Kirby the soldier. Unexpectedly, forcefully. "Gimme the clucking fire numbers, you lardhead!"

Automatically Saunders responded. "Thirty-two and thirty-three."

Quickly, ignoring the fire around him, Keeno shucked off his jacket and shirt. Then like a bony-shouldered little eel, he dove into the culvert pipe. In a moment he was bellying down its length, hands and feet splashing in the thin trickle of water. The pipe shivered from the shells pounding the road above, but the boy kept on moving. Saunders, aghast, watched him. Anybody else would have been too big to go through that pipe. What was the little hammerhead going to do?

Saunders raised his head cautiously, saw Keeno spill out of the end of the culvert and grab up Kirby's radio. Wriggling and darting, the boy kept deep in the weeds along the stream, the antenna of the radio whipping above his head.

That gutsy little Limey, Saunders breathed. *That gutsy little kid! Look at him go!* Because plainly Keeno was running to where he could get positive transmission to battalion. He was their only hope for help.

Then Saunders, the saliva suddenly sour in his mouth, lost sight of the boy in another burst of shellfire. *Oh, Lord,* he prayed silently. *Let him make it. Let him make it.*

The artillery fire thickened in the road again. With a great ringing of gongs in his ears, Saunders felt a giant rabbit punch catch him in the back of the neck. Struggling to open his mouth to protest, he felt himself slipping down, down, down into a great shiny pool of darkness. . . .

As from a great distance, Saunders climbed his way up to a yellowing daylight, and opened his eyes. Doc was squatting over him, mouth in an anxious pucker. "Hey, Sarge," he said softly. "You feel okay? You been out for an hour. You got a little concussion. Here, let me check your eyes."

Doc thumbed his eyelids, looking for the pupil pinpoints that would signify real damage, then said, "Looks okay. How you feel?"

Saunders sat up tentatively. "Okay, I guess. Little shaken up. How're we doing?" He looked around hurriedly, sensing in spite of the splintery sensation in his bones that the military situation had changed. The squad position looked different, too.

A number of poorly dressed men in civilian clothes squatted in the road, gulping K rations. Of course. Refugees from the Wesel slave-labor camp. Kirby leaned back against the embankment, a first-aid pack baled on to his shoulder with hasty loops. Nelson and the Dunn twins herded a dozen Krauts toward the road, their helmets discarded, the long hair they always wore —in contrast to the American idea of short sanitary haircuts for soldiers—now spiky and disarrayed where they clasped hands on their heads. Their eyes had the shocked vacuous stare prisoners took on. They moved with hesitant tentative movements, obviously afraid of what might happen to them now. Carefully, they avoided the laborers. Caje was sitting on the breastworks, facing the road. "Aha, Sergeant," he hailed Saunders. "Goofing off when there is excitement, hey?"

"Guess so, Caje. How we doing?"

Caje waved a hand toward Hill 219. "Objective secured. K Company has passed through. Our platoon is in reserve. For the moment, the battle is over."

Saunders grimaced. Some counterattack. He'd conked out for most of it. "Where are Littlejohn and Brock?"

"Policing up out in front. They're looking for somebody."

"What did I miss?"

Nobody said anything for a minute. Caje looked at Doc, Kirby closed his eyes. The prisoners moved down the road with a shuffling sound, their hobnailed boots raking the gravel. Saunders blinked. This was the last chance he was going to get to square away the Keeno business. He sensed it, clearly and more sharply than he sensed the ache seated deep in the back of his neck. His last conscious picture had been Keeno ducking through the weeds, radio in hand, skinny arms flailing. That gutsy little kid. He cut it for the squad when nobody else could. Well, Chip Saunders wasn't a guy afraid to admit he was wrong, especially when somehow they'd all come through the mill one more time.

"Where's Keeno?" Saunders asked the question crisply. "I had him figured wrong, didn't I? He was the one brought K Company in, wasn't he?"

That started them all talking at once but Caje got hold of the conversational ball. "You should have seen him, Sergeant. He got through on the radio, called in artillery fire, then went back and got the lieutenant and some help. What do you think of that?"

"You know what I think of that. Where is he? I want to shake him by the hand."

Caje's eyes twinkled, Kirby grinned a little, Doc smiled for the first time in a week. And as he looked at them, Saunders knew he didn't have to say any more. Whatever had been between them was now laid to rest forever; they were one for all and all for one now, just like the soldiers in the kid's story. Saunders leaned back for a moment. Maybe that was the place to leave it; sentiment didn't come easy to any of them. But he had to square it with Keeno. He owed the kid that much. "So where's Keeno now? Is he really okay, Caje?"

"Number One. Take a look." Caje jerked a thumb toward the road bending in from Hill 219.

Making a slight column of dust a loaded jeep was chugging toward them. As it came nearer, Saunders recognized it as the company jeep with Davis at the wheel, Littlejohn and Brock perched in the back, two people he couldn't recognize jammed in beside the driver. Then, as the jeep drew closer, Saunders saw who the two people were. In that same moment he knew what he had

to do. He knew exactly what he had to do.

"Caje, come on over with me. Doc, lend me a knife or something sharp. Bayonet's okay."

Doc looked curious but handed Saunders a small penknife. Saunders moved stiffly up to the crown of the road as the jeep pulled up. Both Brock and Littlejohn started talking at once, Keeno and the dark-faced civilian beside him staring apprehensively at Saunders.

"Hold it, you guys. I know who this is. It's Keeno's father. From the Wesel camp." Without waiting for a reply, Saunders reached out and shook hands. "Monseer Quineaux," he said, gripping the skinny fingers, not caring whether the man understood English or not, only wanting to tell him something to get that haunted look out of his sunken eyes. "Your boy's a fine soldier and a hero. I wish we had a hundred like him."

Then Saunders took Keeno's hand, saying, "Keeno, you did a good job for us when the going was tough." As the squad members closed in around him, Saunders went on. "You showed us

you knew the one rule we go by better than anybody else. You helped your buddies when they
needed it most. So, to tell you I know I was wrong
about you, and to tell you how much the squad
and I appreciate what you did, I want to give
you something."

He turned to Caje. "Loan me these for a while,
Caje, do you mind?" Saunders opened Doc's penknife and started to snip the Pfc stripes off Caje's
sleeves.

"Hold it, Sarge. Just a minute." Caje burrowed
in his jacket pocket and came out with two Pfc
stripes curling in his thumb and finger. Grinning
like a toothpaste ad, he handed them to Saunders.
"Remember these? I saved them that day in the
tent. They'd be better."

"That they would." Saunders took the stripes,
and very carefully placed them in the palm of
Keeno's hand, then closed the frail fingers over
them with his own big hand. "Put 'em back on,
Keeno. If anybody in this outfit is a first-class
soldier, you are."

Keeno looked down at his hand, then at Saunders, looked at his father, then back at Saunders. Then he smiled, slowly, and the movement hid whatever it was glistening in his black eyes. "Righto, Sergeant," he said softly. "I'll see they never need come off again."

There was a ragged cheer from the squad. They all crowded around the jeep to slap Keeno on the back and shake hands with him and his father.

Somebody poked Saunders in the ribs as he stepped out of the way. It was Kirby, a little shaky, but there. "Lucky kid, ain't he, Sarge? He's got what—seven, no eight, fathers now."

Saunders was silent for a beat. He was thinking that here was the spirit that made the squad go. God willing, it'd get them through the war. And somehow, deep down, he knew they'd make it. But he couldn't get all that into words. So he simply said, "Yeah, man. You better believe it."

Whitman CLASSICS

Five Little Peppers Midway

Mrs. Wiggs of the
Cabbage Patch

Fifty Famous Fairy Tales

Eight Cousins

Little Women

Black Beauty

Five Little Peppers and
How They Grew

Treasure Island

Heidi

The Call of the Wild

Tom Sawyer

Beautiful Joe

Adventures of Sherlock Holmes

Little Lame Prince

Here are some of the best-loved stories of all time.
Delightful ... intriguing ... never-to-be-forgotten
tales that you will read again and again. Start
your own home library of WHITMAN CLASSICS
so that you'll always have exciting books at your
finger tips.

Whitman ADVENTURE and MYSTERY Books

Adventure Stories for GIRLS and BOYS ...

TIMBER TRAIL RIDERS
The Long Trail North
The Texas Tenderfoot
The Luck of Black Diamond
Mystery of the Hollywood Horse
The Mysterious Dude

POWER BOYS SERIES
The Haunted Skyscraper
The Flying Skeleton

DONNA PARKER
In Hollywood
At Cherrydale
Special Agent
On Her Own
A Spring to Remember
Mystery at Arawak
Takes a Giant Step

TROY NESBIT SERIES
Sand Dune Pony
Diamond Cave Mystery
Indian Mummy Mystery
Mystery at Rustlers' Fort

New Stories About Your Television Favorites ...

Dr. Kildare
Assigned to Trouble
The Magic Key

Janet Lennon at Camp Calamity

Walt Disney's Annette
Mystery at Smugglers' Cove
Desert Inn Mystery
Sierra Summer
Mystery at Moonstone Bay
Mystery at Medicine Wheel

Combat! The Counterattack

The Beverly Hillbillies

Lassie
Secret of the Summer
Forbidden Valley
Mystery at Blackberry Bog

Lucy and the Madcap Mystery

Patty Duke and Mystery Mansion